★ 108課綱、全民英檢初／中級適用

Basic Reading：
悅讀養成 二版

附解析夾冊

三民英語編輯小組　彙編

三民書局

序

知識，就是希望；閱讀，就是力量。

在這個資訊爆炸的時代，應該如何選擇真正有用的資訊來吸收？
在考場如戰場的競爭壓力之下，應該如何儲備實力，漂亮地面對挑戰？
身為地球村的一分子，應該如何增進英語實力，與世界接軌？

學習英文的目的，就是要讓自己在這個資訊爆炸的時代之中，突破語言的藩籬，站在吸收新知的制高點之上，以閱讀獲得力量，以知識創造希望！

針對在英文閱讀中可能面對的挑戰，我們費心規劃 Reading Power 系列叢書，希望在學習英語的路上助你一臂之力，讓你輕鬆閱讀、快樂學習。

誠摯希望在學習英語的路上，這套 Reading Power 系列叢書將伴隨你找到閱讀的力量，發揮知識的光芒！

給讀者的話

　　對許多人來說，閱讀英文文章可能是件辛苦的事，但在許多重要考試中，閱讀能力卻是得分關鍵。若無法理解文意，在作答閱讀測驗題目時，更是難上加難、雪上加霜。因此，平時即應養成閱讀的習慣，並試做題目，以提升閱讀能力。一般來說，各類英文考試的閱讀測驗題型約可分為以下五種：

1. 理解文章要旨 (Main Idea)
2. 掃描文章細節 (Details)
3. 推論文章之引申意義 (Inference)
4. 辨認文章中之指涉詞 (Reference)
5. 判斷文章中之字義 (Vocabulary in Context)

　　有鑑於此，本書針對此五大題型設計閱讀測驗，並精選文章中單字或片語讓讀者做字詞選填之練習，希望讀者透過這些內容，能夠增加閱讀英文文章的速度、加強字彙量以及對題型的熟練程度。書中各回以文章篇幅依序排列，期望讀者由短篇文章開始，循序漸進熟悉與各大考試字數相當之文章，經由反覆練習，以達到得心應手之效。

　　此外，本書附上每回之全文翻譯、重點試題說明和難字提示，方便讀者自修。提醒讀者不要急著看翻譯解答，在練習完一至二回後再核對答案，如此經過這五十篇的訓練後，相信讀者已然養成獨立閱讀、分析英文文章，並強化對文章理解、引申、推理、判斷的能力。

　　本書之編寫力求完善，但難免有疏漏之處，望讀者與各界賢達隨時賜教。

三民英語編輯小組　謹誌

Table of Contents

圖片來源：Shutterstock

$\mathcal{B}$asic Reading
悅讀養成

READ

BOOK

Unit 1   A Chain of Life

Once upon a time, the farmers in a small village were worried about one thing: the eagles were eating all of their chickens on their farms. They couldn't think of other ways than killing the eagles to save their chickens. So, they rounded up all the eagles and killed them.

But soon they had another problem: their fields were overrun with field mice, which were eating away at their crops! The farmers didn't know that eagles ate both chickens and field mice—in fact, more field mice than chickens. It turned out that killing the eagles **upset** the balance of nature.

It is also true when people first move into a place. They often cut their way through the wild trees and grass, not knowing that many animals live on these plants. If animals don't have enough plants to eat, they will die or have to leave. The balance of nature can be easily disturbed. We need to do all we can to keep this balance and protect the Earth for the generations to come.

Reading Comprehension: Choose the best answer for each question.

_____ 1. What's the article mainly about?

(A) Eagles are dangerous.

(B) Wild animals don't have enough plants to eat.

(C) Killing eagles will upset the balance of nature.

(D) We should try our best to keep the balance of nature.

_____ 2. Why did the farmers kill the eagles?

(A) Because they ate up their chickens.

(B) Because they ate away at their crops.

(C) Because there were too many mice.

(D) Because there were too many eagles.

_____ 3. What happened after the farmers killed all the eagles?

(A) Mice appeared in their fields.

(B) There were too many chickens.

(C) Other wild animals died or had to leave.

(D) Other wild animals didn't have enough food to eat.

_____ 4. The word "upset" in paragraph 2 means making _____.

(A) a plan, or a situation go wrong

(B) someone feel unhappy or annoyed

(C) something fall out of bed

(D) someone feel sick or ill

_____ 5. Which of the following is true?

(A) The eagles ate more chickens than mice.

(B) The balance of nature can be easily upset.

(C) Killing the eagles can help keep the balance of nature.

(D) The farmers killed all the eagles to save field mice and their crops.

Try it! Fill in each blank with the correct word. Make changes if necessary.

think of	in fact	turn out	balance	generation

1. Mr. White tries to strike a _____ between work and family.

2. Everything will _____ to be all right. Don't worry.

3. You can see three _____ of Ivy's family in the photo: her grandparents, her parents, and her brothers.

4. Tom looks young, but _____, he is over 40 years old.

5. Yesterday, Jessie met a high school classmate, but she couldn't _____ his name.

Short-form Video Trends

In today's fast-paced world, short-form videos shine as the stars of our digital entertainment. They typically last less than a minute! Thanks to smartphones and apps like TikTok and Instagram, these short-form videos have attracted millions of views. Almost anyone with a smartphone can create and share these videos easily.

These short clips serve a range of purposes, from entertainment to education. Creators can make short-form videos to make viewers laugh or show off their talents like dancing or singing. Also, some can even give quick tips on cooking, DIY projects, or share news updates. One great thing about these short-form videos is that they can **go viral**. That means they spread really fast across the Internet when people share them. This can get millions of people to watch. For the people who make the videos, it can mean becoming famous and even making money from ads.

However, some people worry that these short-form videos might make us have shorter attention spans or not think as much. Others are concerned about mean or harmful content spreading. So, it's important to be careful and use these videos in a positive way.

In sum, short-form videos have changed how we make, watch, and share videos online. They're super popular, and it looks like they're going to keep being a big part of how we do things on the Internet.

Reading Comprehension: Choose the best answer for each question.

_____ 1. What is the passage mainly about?

    (A) The comparison between TikTok and Instagram.

    (B) The negative impacts of short-form videos on kids.

    (C) The challenges creators face in making short videos.

(D) The popularity of short-formed videos in the digital era.

_____ 2. What does "go viral" mean in the second paragraph?

　　(A) See clearly.　　　　　　　(B) Spread quickly.

　　(C) View easily.　　　　　　　(D) Post regularly.

_____ 3. What is the purpose of this passage?

　　(A) To highlight the success of short-form creators.

　　(B) To criticize the negative impact of short-form videos.

　　(C) To point out the worries and advantages of short-form videos.

　　(D) To show how people use short-form videos to promote products.

_____ 4. Which of the following best describes the author's attitude toward the future of short-form videos?

　　(A) Angry.　　　(B) Doubtful.　　　(C) Hopeful.　　　(D) Conservative.

_____ 5. According to the passage, what are some concerns people have about short-form videos?

　　(A) They may make us spend more time on the Internet.

　　(B) They may promote negative content.

　　(C) They may affect the quality of the picture.

　　(D) They may limit our use of mobile devices.

Try it! Fill in each blank with the correct word. Make changes if necessary.

talent	entertainment	attention	harmful	concerned

1. The guitar player showed his _____ for music at the charity event.
2. We should avoid anything _____ to our health, like drinking too much sugary drinks.
3. Parents are always _____ about their children's safety.
4. It's important to pay close _____ to what the teacher is saying in class.
5. I enjoy various forms of _____ , such as watching movies, playing games, or listening to music.

Unit 3 "Go Fly a Kite" in Japan

The Japanese tradition of kite-flying is over 1,000 years old. Kites in Japan come in various shapes of animals from bats to bees or birds. Most of the kites are decorated with pictures.

When it comes to kites, the Japanese have many fun stories to tell. One is about a thief who wanted to steal gold by using a huge kite, because the gold was kept at the top of a high tower. On a windy night, he rode on the kite to the tower top, and with his friend's help, they took the gold away. Another is about a father and a son who were in trouble on an island near Japan. The son finally made it to Japan by his father's handmade kite.

Also, there are kite matches among young people, in which they try to cut off others' kite strings. The match lasts until there is only one kite left in the sky.

Reading Comprehension: Choose the best answer for each question.

_____ 1. The article is mainly about _____ .
    (A) kite matches
    (B) different shapes of kites
    (C) Japanese stories about stealing gold
    (D) the tradition of kite-flying in Japan

_____ 2. In Japan, kites are made in the shapes of _____ .
    (A) bats   (B) bees
    (C) birds   (D) All of the above.

_____ 3. In the Japanese story, why did the thief use a kite to steal gold?
    (A) Because he loved kite matches.
    (B) Because kites came in various shapes.
    (C) Because he liked to ride kites very much.
    (D) Because the gold was kept at the top of a high tower.

_____ 4. In the kite matches, people have to _____ .

(A) ride kites

(B) tell fun stories

(C) cut off others' kite strings

(D) decorate their kites with pictures

_____ 5. Which of the following is true?

(A) In Japan, kite matches are popular among the elderly.

(B) A kite match ends when all the kites fly in the sky.

(C) In the Japanese stories, people rode kites to steal or escape.

(D) The Japanese tradition of kite-flying is less than 1,000 years old.

Try it! Fill in each blank with the correct word. Make changes if necessary.

various	decorate	when it comes to	make it	cut off

1. _____ 100-meter sprints, Lucy is as good as her sister.

2. Two of her fingers were _____ in the accident.

3. Yesterday, they _____ the hall with flowers to make it more beautiful.

4. As long as you work hard, you will _____ .

5. You can buy _____ kinds of products in the supermarket.

Unit 4 The Rise of Digital Nomads

A digital nomad is someone who works from wherever they want. They use mobile devices like smartphones and laptops to communicate and work with their team. They can even choose when, where, and how they work. Unlike regular workers, digital nomads lead an independent lifestyle.

Thanks to new technology, digital nomads don't have to work in a traditional office. They arrange their own schedules and can pick the best place to work. Some like to work in the morning and take a long break later, while others prefer working late at night. It's all up to them.

However, there are some challenges too. For example, finding good Wi-Fi in remote places is not easy! In addition, when digital nomads work with people in different countries, dealing with time differences can be tricky. Most importantly, digital nomads often face challenges in finding the true work-life balance because the lines between their work and personal life are not clear. In fact, digital nomads like to go to places like Bali, Chiang Mai, and Berlin. These places are great because of their low cost of living and reliable Internet connection.

As technology gets better, more people are likely to choose the digital nomad lifestyle. It's like having a job that lets you be free and explore new places. The future of work is changing, and lots of people are excited to try out this flexible way of living.

 Reading Comprehension: Choose the best answer for each question.

_____ 1. What is the passage mainly about?

(A) The future of digital nomads.   (B) The lifestyle of digital nomads.

(C) Successful digital nomads.   (D) The history of digital nomads.

_____ 2. Which of the following is true about digital nomads?

　　(A) They prefer to work in a regular office.

　　(B) They like to explore new places without working.

　　(C) They work remotely using mobile devices.

　　(D) They avoid using smartphones and laptops.

_____ 3. Where does this passage most likely appear?

　　(A) In a business magazine focused on remote work trends.

　　(B) In a handbook for office managers.

　　(C) On an ad featuring popular countries for traveling alone.

　　(D) On a website of a software company.

_____ 4. How do digital nomads arrange their work schedules?

　　(A) They work in the morning only.

　　(B) They work late at night only.

　　(C) They work during regular office hours.

　　(D) They work whenever they feel like it.

_____ 5. Why do digital nomads choose places like Bali and Berlin to work?

　　(A) Because of their nice weather.

　　(B) Because of their good Wi-Fi.

　　(C) Because of their modern office spaces.

　　(D) Because of their beautiful nature views.

Try it!　Fill in each blank with the correct word. Make changes if necessary.

explore	arrange	flexible	digital	remote

1. Mia lives in a(n) _____ village which is far away from the urban area.

2. _____ technology has changed the way we get information.

3. I need to _____ a meeting with my boss to discuss the project in detail.

4. We went on a tour to _____ the beautiful scenery near the lake.

5. Ed's work schedule is _____, so he can adjust his work hours to fit his needs.

Unit 5　Unlocking the Mystery of Doors Unlocked

It is estimated that 2 million people in the U.K. leave their houses unlocked when they go out. This act of forgetfulness is not limited to those living in the countryside. People living in cities can be just as careless. Almost one out of ten Londoners admit to leaving their doors, back doors in particular, unlocked. There are several reasons why people leave their doors unlocked.

Quite sure that their neighbors will keep an eye on their property, 18% of the people say they'd leave without locking their doors. Another 18% say they feel safe because they live in a neighborhood where crimes are not so common; 60% admit to simply being forgetful, according to a survey by Halifax Home Insurance. Some 17 million people also think it is OK to leave their houses unlocked while they are inside despite the fact that almost 55% of burglaries happen in the houses with people inside.

Reading Comprehension: Choose the best answer for each question.

_____ 1. The article mainly talks about _____ .
  (A) why many people in the U.K. are forgetful
  (B) how many burglaries happen in the houses with people inside
  (C) why many people in the U.K. leave their houses unlocked
  (D) how careless people living in cities can be just as those living in the countryside

_____ 2. _____% of the people admit that they just forget to lock the door before going out.
  (A) 17　　　　　　(B) 18　　　　　　(C) 55　　　　　　(D) 60

_____ 3. _____% of the people leave their houses unlocked because the crime rate in their neighborhoods is low.
  (A) 17　　　　　　(B) 18　　　　　　(C) 55　　　　　　(D) 60

_____ 4. _____ million people leave their houses unlocked when they are at home.

(A) 2   (B) 10   (C) 17   (D) 18

_____ 5. Which of the following is the reason why people leave their houses unlocked?

(A) They are not at home.

(B) They seldom use back doors.

(C) Crimes are common in their neighborhoods.

(D) Their neighbors will watch their houses for them.

Try it! Fill in each blank with the correct word. Make changes if necessary.

estimate	admit	in particular	property	crime

1. The cart is the old man's only _____; he owns nothing else.

2. William _____ to having lied and said he was sorry.

3. It is _____ that it will take two years to restore the old church.

4. The man has committed some serious _____, such as murder and robbery.

5. The Oscar winner owed his achievement to lots of people, his wife _____.

Unit 6　Korean Soaps Sweep China

　　Korean TV series now have lots of fans in China. They are aired during prime time and many people hurry home just to watch them. What about those who can't make it? No worries—there're the reruns! Stories of love triangles, everyday family affairs, kings and queens, and doctors are very popular. Fans say they love their good-looking idols, the latest fashions they wear, and so on.

　　Korean TV series also enjoy popularity among those born in the 40s and 50s, only for a different reason. Morals, such as respect for the elderly and traditions, are what attract them.

　　The audiences do have their complaints, though. Some say they hate it when these shows drag, and others are sick of lovesick couples or endless family fights. However, most people agree that with more shows to choose from, they have a lot more to talk about at the dinner table.

Reading Comprehension: Choose the best answer for each question.

_____ 1. The article mainly talks about _____ .

    (A) the latest fashions   (B) Korean TV series

    (C) the respect for traditions   (D) prime time TV programs

_____ 2. Many Korean TV series are about _____ .

    (A) stories of love triangles   (B) everyday family affairs

    (C) kings and queens   (D) All of the above.

_____ 3. The reason why Korean TV series attract those born in the 40s and 50s is _____ .

    (A) the morals   (B) the good-looking actors

    (C) the latest fashions the actors wear   (D) the subject of endless family fights

_____ 4. What do the audiences complain about Korean TV series?

(A) The shows go on for too long.

(B) The subject is always about lovesick couples.

(C) The subject is always about endless family fights.

(D) All of the above.

_____ 5. Which of the following is true?

(A) Korean TV series are popular only among teenagers.

(B) If people can't watch Korean TV series during prime time, they can watch the reruns.

(C) "Prime time" means the time when the smallest number of people are watching television.

(D) Some audiences are sick of Korean TV series because they are always about kings and queens.

Try it! Fill in each blank with the correct word. Make changes if necessary.

affair   morals   tradition   idol   audience

1. The little girl screamed when she saw the popular _____ .

2. When to quit is my personal _____ ; it is none of your business.

3. When the dancer finished his performance, the _____ stood up and clapped heartily.

4. The readers can get the _____ and customs of the Tang Dynasty from the book.

5. Eating mooncakes has been a _____ in Taiwan during the Moon Festival.

Unit 7　The United World School

Students in the United World School come from all over the world. In this school students study and spend their free time together. The school believes this will help them grow up to be knowledgeable, caring, and friendly.

A special "United Nations" show is put on annually. Students are encouraged to bring to the show things that are characteristic of their own cultures. Before the show, there's a cultural exchange among the students. The school is convinced that by doing so, the gap between different cultures will be bridged.

Students in this school can make their own decisions in some **respects**. The senior members can dress any clothes they like in their ways while the junior wear the uniform of their choice. However, there are still two preconditions: no expensive accessories and no offense against others with your outfit.

There's no way to satisfy all people. Unless students embrace cultures besides their own, there's no other way to make the world wonderful.

 Reading Comprehension: Choose the best answer for each question.

_____ 1. What is the main idea of the article?
　　(A) There's no way to satisfy all people.
　　(B) The United World School is a good school.
　　(C) Never wear offensive clothes or accessories.
　　(D) Embracing other cultures, we can make the world wonderful.

_____ 2. The United World School wants to help the students to _____ .

　　(A) embrace cultures besides their own

　　(B) show things that are characteristic of their own cultures

　　(C) grow up to be knowledgeable, caring, and friendly

　　(D) All of the above.

_____ 3. _____ is meant to help bridge cultural gaps.

　　(A) The "United Nations" show and the cultural exchange before it

　　(B) A casual dress code for the senior students

　　(C) A conservative dress code for the junior students

　　(D) All of the above.

_____ 4. The word "respect" in paragraph 3 means _____ .

　　(A) a certain aspect of something

　　(B) polite behavior toward someone

　　(C) a feeling of admiration for someone

　　(D) having a very good opinion of something

_____ 5. Which of the following is true?

　　(A) The "United Nations" show is put on twice a year.

　　(B) Students in the United World School come from different cultures.

　　(C) Students in the United World School seldom spend their free time together.

　　(D) Senior students in the United World School are allowed to wear costly accessories to school.

Try it! Fill in each blank with the correct word. Make changes if necessary.

embrace	encourage	characteristic	exchange	convinced

1. In Taiwan, hot and humid weather is _____ of summer.

2. Ella _____ her mother on Mother's Day.

3. We don't believe Bob, but Cindy is _____ that Bob is innocent.

4. The success may _____ Dr. Wu to further his experiment.

5. Owen gave me a book. In _____ , I gave him a magazine.

Unit 8　Sound Speed vs. Light Speed

When did you last throw a stone into water? Do you know how waves develop? They form when the stone touches the water. Then they start spreading.

Sound takes time to travel in air, like waves in water. Sound travels as vibrations move among molecules, and it needs a medium, like air, to travel. Sometimes we can't see or hear a train coming, but if we put our ears onto the rails, we actually can hear the sound of a moving train. It tells us that sound travels faster through solids, such as wood and metal, than through air.

However, light doesn't need any medium to travel through. You're likely to have detected lightning comes before a **crack** of thunder. This is because light travels a great deal faster than sound does. Each second, light can travel over 300,000,000 meters while sound about 340 meters. That is why you see something happen before the sound comes to your ears.

Reading Comprehension: Choose the best answer for each question.

_____ 1. The article is mainly about _____ .
  (A) how light travels
  (B) how waves develop
  (C) why sound travels more slowly than light
  (D) why throwing a stone into water can cause waves

_____ 2. As vibrations move among molecules and waves spread in water, sound
  _____ .
  (A) takes time to travel　　　　(B) travels a great distance
  (C) travels at 340 meters per second　　(D) comes before a crack of thunder

_____ 3. The word "crack" in paragraph 3 means _____ .

    (A) a sudden loud noise

    (B) a narrow space or opening

    (C) a sharp blow that can be heard

    (D) a line on the surface of something when it is broken

_____ 4. Light travels at _____ .

    (A) 340 meters per second   (B) 340 meters per minute

    (C) 300,000,000 meters per minute   (D) 300,000,000 meters per second

_____ 5. Which of the following is true?

    (A) A thunderclap comes before lightning.

    (B) We hear sound before seeing what happened.

    (C) Sound travels a great deal faster than light does.

    (D) None of the above.

Try it!   Fill in each blank with the correct word. Make changes if necessary.

develop	distance	be likely to	detect	a great deal

1. There is a _____ of 500 meters between the library and the bus stop.

2. Dogs can _____ sounds that humans cannot hear.

3. The small town has _____ into a big city.

4. After taking the medicine, the patient is _____ better now.

5. The sky turns dark; it _____ rain soon.

17

Unit 9 Body Talk

We think about people in different ways when we see their body language. Also, our body language would express ourselves. More than what we say, our faces, hands, and eyes talk a lot about us.

The face is very important in showing our inner ideas. The face can express our feelings of disinterest or stress. Often a smile can show good feelings to others and make others think that we are warm and friendly.

Eyes can also express the feelings in our mind. A hard look can mean interest, anger, or fear. Not looking directly in the eyes can mean that one is shy. Regular eye contact shows that one is comfortable and at ease.

Open hand movements make one appear honest. The right hand movements can add importance to what one says. Moderate hand movements can make one look interested, while too many movements of the hands express **tension** and stress.

Our body movements express what is going on in our mind and can let others know what we are thinking. Therefore, using appropriate body language is important.

Reading Comprehension: Choose the best answer for each question.

_____ 1. According to the article, our faces _____.

    (A) say nothing about our true feelings

    (B) can tell others what our inner ideas are

    (C) only show stress and disinterest

    (D) make people think we are warm and friendly

_____ 2. If you talk to people without looking them in the eye, people will probably think _____ .

(A) you don't like them   (B) you are angry

(C) you don't want to talk to them   (D) you are shy

_____ 3. In the fourth paragraph, the meaning of the word "tension" is closest to _____ .

(A) nervousness   (B) disinterest   (C) movement   (D) importance

_____ 4. Which of the following about hand movements is true?

(A) If people talk without hands open, they are not honest.

(B) A person talking with many hand movements might get worried easily.

(C) Only the movements of right hands can make what people say important.

(D) If a person tells a lie, he or she will move hands quickly.

_____ 5. What is the main idea of the article?

(A) If we use body language, we don't need to talk at all.

(B) The more body language we use, the better we understand each other.

(C) We need to practice smiling because it is the best language.

(D) We can let others know how we feel by using body language at the right time.

Try it! Fill in each blank with the correct word. Make changes if necessary.

at ease	appear	moderate	tension	appropriate

1. It's not _____ to say rude things at a formal occasion.
2. She _____ calm after arguing with her boyfriend.
3. Mary looked _____ after she knew her brother was safe.
4. My mother was under great _____ because of her busy life.
5. The test sheet is for students of _____ ability.

Unit 10 Air Pollution Is "in the Air"

Scientists have long expressed worries about air pollution affecting Nature. Concerns are even raised that indoor air isn't safer than outdoor air. People who stay in buildings for a long time may feel dizzy, sleepy, and may catch a cold easily. This condition is called "Sick Building Syndrome."

According to scientists, houses of today are the source of some kinds of pollution. It wasn't until the early 1970s that people were aware of this problem. Since builders wanted to cut back on the budgets, they chose artificial materials to put up buildings, putting the dwellers in danger of inhaling harmful gases given off by the materials.

The search for solutions to the problem was underway amid the worsening of it; some scientists later found out the answer actually lay in Nature—green plants.

Scientists think that plant leaves can reduce pollutants while releasing oxygen. Studies on plants find different plants absorb different chemicals. Therefore, the more kinds of plants people grow, the better air quality will be.

Reading Comprehension: Choose the best answer for each question.

_____ 1. The article is mainly about _____ .
  (A) pollution of all sorts
  (B) air pollution affecting Nature
  (C) the use of artificial building materials
  (D) the pollutants given off by building materials

_____ 2. Why are houses home to pollution?

    (A) Because of the use of energy.

    (B) Because of the plants grown indoors.

    (C) Because of outdoor air pollution.

    (D) Because of the use of artificial building materials.

_____ 3. Some builders used artificial building materials because they _____.

    (A) wanted to cut down on the budgets

    (B) worried about air pollution affecting Nature

    (C) found plants could absorb different chemicals

    (D) were afraid that dwellers might inhale harmful gases

_____ 4. What can be the solution to the problem of indoor pollutants?

    (A) Chemicals.   (B) Green plants.

    (C) New forms of energy.   (D) New building materials.

_____ 5. Which of the following is true?

    (A) Some plants can absorb chemicals.

    (B) Some plants can release harmful gases.

    (C) Only a few kinds of plants can make indoor air quality better.

    (D) Before the 1970s, people had already become aware that houses were home to some pollution.

Try it!   Fill in each blank with the correct word. Make changes if necessary.

      express   pollution   affect   reduce   absorb

1. What parents do and say _____ their children greatly. It has a great effect on how their children act or think.

2. By day, plants _____ carbon dioxide and discharge oxygen.

3. After winning the game, the players _____ thanks to their coach.

4. Larry wanted to _____ his weight from 90 to 70 kilograms.

5. The increasing number of cars has caused serious air _____.

Unit 11 Celebrities and Social Anxiety

Living with social anxiety can make you feel alone, especially in the age of social media. On places such as Facebook and Instagram, you may see many pictures of people having fun, but you never know what's happening in their lives. Actually, some celebrities suffer from social anxiety and have openly talked about their struggles with it. This shows that such challenges are not as uncommon as you think.

Naomi Osaka, a famous Japanese tennis player known for beating Serena Williams, has been struggling with social anxiety. She's a tennis icon but had to protect her mental health by canceling press interviews during the French Open. Osaka opened up about her depression and **introverted nature**. She had to wear headphones at tournaments to **cope with** social anxiety. After her announcement, she received support from fellow athletes.

Kim Basinger, a well-known actress, also battled social anxiety. She often felt extreme fear and even had a nervous breakdown when asked to read aloud in class. Basinger struggled to find words during her Oscar speech and tried to discuss her anxiety and panic attacks. Therapy helped, but challenges remain.

These celebrities, loved by millions, show that social anxiety is normal. You can seek help when needed. By sharing your experiences, you may help others facing similar challenges. Remember, it's okay to talk about your feelings, and there's always support available.

Reading Comprehension: Choose the best answer for each question.

_____ 1. Where does this passage most likely appear?

    (A) On an ad featuring contemporary arts.

    (B) On a website of an art gallery.

    (C) In a booklet on Oscar winners.

    (D) In a mental health awareness campaign.

_____ 2. According to the passage, how did Naomi Osaka deal with social anxiety during tournaments?

(A) By canceling press interviews. (B) By avoiding social media.

(C) By participating in therapy. (D) By wearing headphones.

_____ 3. What can be inferred from the passage about Kim Basinger's experience with social anxiety?

(A) She never faced challenges during her Oscar speech.

(B) Therapy completely resolved her social anxiety.

(C) She struggled to read aloud in class because of extreme fear.

(D) She overcame her anxiety with ease.

_____ 4. What does the author mean by "introverted nature" in the passage?

(A) A shy and reserved personality. (B) An outgoing and sociable friend.

(C) A lack of interest in sports. (D) A preference for press interviews.

_____ 5. What does the phrase "cope with" in the second paragraph most likely mean?

(A) Struggle. (B) Manage. (C) Avoid. (D) Ignore.

Try it! Fill in each blank with the correct word. Make changes if necessary.

breakdown	celebrity	support	struggle	share

1. Famous people like actors and singers are often called _____.
2. Real life is full of challenges, and we must _____ to grow stronger.
3. Sometimes when things are very hard, people might have a _____.
4. Sarah found an interesting article and _____ it with her friends online.
5. It's important to have friends and family who give us _____ when we face difficulties.

Unit 12 Your Thinking Is Your Everything

Exactly how do successful people think differently from others? What drives them towards success? Interviews and studies have shown that successful people do have a couple of qualities in common.

To begin with, those who succeed seldom look down on someone who fails. They believe that if he or she keeps trying hard, one day he or she will succeed, too. They also believe that their futures are shaped by themselves. They accept that not everything in their lives is in their control, but they can choose how they think and what they do.

The most important thing that sets successful people apart may be—they live with a strong sense of purpose. They may spend a long time looking for what they are born to do, but they feel the need to do what they believe in. Having a purpose in life **means the world to them**. Also, successful people are no quitters. Once they set their hearts on something, they are ready to take on whatever challenge that comes their way.

Reading Comprehension: Choose the best answer for each question.

_____ 1. The article is mainly about _____ .
    (A) what leads people to success
    (B) what jobs successful people choose to do
    (C) how successful people treat someone who fails
    (D) how successful people get everything in their control

_____ 2. Why do successful people seldom look down on someone who fails?
    (A) Because they have failed before.
    (B) Because they can help him or her to shape the future.
    (C) Because they can help him or her to get everything under control.
    (D) Because they believe he or she will succeed someday as well.

_____ 3. What mainly sets successful people apart is their _____ .

(A) belief in hard work   (B) strong sense of purpose

(C) strong sense of responsibility   (D) belief in themselves

_____ 4. Which of the following about successful people is NOT true?

(A) They never give up what they've planned to do.

(B) It may take them a great deal of time to find a purpose in life.

(C) They have certain qualities in common which set them apart from others.

(D) When challenge comes their way, they always change their minds.

_____ 5. The phrase "mean the world to someone" in the last paragraph means

_____ .

(A) being very important to someone   (B) being very famous or popular

(C) having lots of experience of life   (D) being very impressive to someone

Try it!   Fill in each blank with the correct word. Make changes if necessary.

a couple of	in common	to begin with	look down on	take on

1. The restaurant was great! _____ , the food was tasty. Then, the service was nice.

2. The doctor advised Bruce not to _____ any more heavy work.

3. We _____ people who always blame others for their own mistakes.

4. Don't worry. We've still got _____ minutes left.

5. They are twins, and they have a lot _____ .

Unit 13　From Shyness to Social Success

Dear Justin,

　　Being shy may be the cause of your problem. You might be too shy to meet new people because you feel you are not attractive enough. I have a few tips to help you build your confidence. All you need to do is prove to your classmates that you are actually an amazing person.

　　The first step to take is to smile. A sincere smile says a lot about your willingness to make friends. Do this regularly, until your classmates become used to it and smile back.

　　Next, try talking to people around you. Start with a casual chat about things in the immediate surroundings. The best time in a day to do this is between classes or during the lunch break. Approach your classmates when they are not busy. It's easier to strike up a conversation when people are by themselves.

　　It takes time to get to know a person and, similarly, it takes time to find someone that you are comfortable being yourself with.

　　Keep practicing these tips, and one day, you'll find yourself attracting people like you have never been.

Uncle Melvin

Reading Comprehension: Choose the best answer for each question.

_____ 1. The article is mainly about _____ .

(A) how to be attractive

(B) how to make new friends

(C) how to become an amazing person

(D) how to overcome the problem of being shy

_____ 2. The article would possibly be found in a _____ .

(A) medical journal   (B) scientific journal

(C) design magazine   (D) newspaper column

_____ 3. Why was Justin shy to meet strangers?

(A) Because he was over-confident.

(B) Because he was not sincere enough.

(C) Because he was unwilling to make friends.

(D) Because he thought he was not attractive enough.

_____ 4. What did Melvin suggest Justin do?

(A) Keep smiling.   (B) Build confidence.

(C) Try to make conversations.   (D) All of the above.

_____ 5. Which of the following is NOT true?

(A) Getting to know a person takes some time.

(B) It's easier to strike up a conversation when people are busy.

(C) Wearing smiles shows one's willingness to make friends.

(D) Starting a conversation with things around you is a good idea.

Try it! Fill in each blank with the correct word. Make changes if necessary.

attractive	confidence	become used to	surroundings	approach

1. I have complete _____ in myself. I believe I can make it.

2. When David _____ the corner, he found a park on the left.

3. They lived in pleasant _____ . Their apartment was nice and cozy.

4. At first, stinky tofu smelt odd to Nicky, but soon he _____ the smell and found it tasty.

5. Julia's smile was so _____ that it caught everyone's eye.

Unit 14 Kiosks

Self-service kiosks help people and businesses with simple tasks. They are able to quickly solve a number of problems and offer many forms of convenience. These machines have been around for a long time. They started as simple vending machines and have developed into the interactive kiosks of today.

Kiosks can reduce the amount of talking between customers and employees. And they are very easy to keep clean. This was important during and after the COVID-19 crisis, as people wanted safe ways of doing things. Some kiosks don't even need to be touched to function, like using a smartphone code to buy something. This is called a touchless experience.

Kiosks are also good for businesses that struggle to find employees. They are simple to use, so businesses can provide good service without needing lots of **staff**. Even helping those who can't use the kiosks requires fewer people than having someone assist every single customer.

For customers, one great thing about self-service kiosks is they shorten waiting times. Instead of waiting in line, you can quickly choose what you want on the kiosk. Many stores have seen a 40% decrease in how long customers have to wait for service. If you know what you want, using a kiosk is quick and keeps the line moving.

No matter what type of business you have, self-service kiosks can make things better. If used correctly, they help a business save money, help customers save time, and make things easier for everyone!

Reading Comprehension: Choose the best answer for each question.

_____ 1. What is the third paragraph mainly about?

(A) Why businesses use self-service kiosks.

(B) How businesses dislike self-service kiosks.

(C) What businesses use to replace self-service kiosks.

(D) When self-service kiosks start to help businesses.

_____ 2. According to the passage, why were self-service kiosks important during COVID-19?

(A) Because they could provide good service with fewer staff.

(B) Because they could avoid wait times.

(C) Because they could provide a touchless experience.

(D) Because they could collect data about customers' habits.

_____ 3. What is the purpose of the passage?

(A) To criticize the use of self-service kiosks.

(B) To describe how kiosks are used in cleaning businesses.

(C) To inform readers about the history of kiosks.

(D) To prove the benefits of self-service kiosks.

_____ 4. What does the word "staff" in the third paragraph most likely mean?

(A) Customers.　　(B) Employees.　　(C) Machines.　　(D) Stores.

_____ 5. Which of the following best describes the author's attitude toward the self-kiosks?

(A) Negative.　　(B) Positive.　　(C) Doubtful.　　(D) Conservative.

Try it!　Fill in each blank with the correct word. Make changes if necessary.

decrease	interactive	task	convenience	touchless

1. The new game is _____. It allows players to talk to characters.

2. The supermarket introduced _____ payment options. Customers can pay without touching money.

3. The _____ in oil prices made many taxi drivers very happy.

4. The to-do list on this app can help you organize _____ efficiently.

5. The _____ of online shopping makes it simple to order our favorite items and have them delivered to our doorsteps with just a few clicks.

Unit 15 Watch Out Behind You

One school in suburban London allows its students to go into town in the afternoon. But there is just one condition: they must be back by 6 p.m. One afternoon, Bob went downtown to catch a movie. When he came back to school, the school gate had already closed. He went to the other side of the campus in the hope of getting in through the back gate. Unfortunately, that one closed, too. Then he saw a window wide open some feet away.

The window led to the school principal's office. Bob poked his head into the room and thought, "**There is not a soul in here.**" He then quickly climbed into the room. Just then he heard a familiar voice, so he hid himself behind an office chair. It was the principal coming in. The principal sat down in the chair and read for an hour. At last, the principal got up from his chair and went towards the door. "Whew! That was close," Bob thought. Just as he stood up to leave, the principal spoke to the chair, "Would you turn off the lights, please?"

Reading Comprehension: Choose the best answer for each question.

_____ 1. The students can go into town in the afternoon as long as they _____.
   (A) go there to catch a movie
   (B) return to school before 6 in the evening
   (C) turn off the lights before leaving
   (D) get in the campus through the back gate

_____ 2. What did Bob go downtown for?
   (A) Shopping.   (B) Watching a film.
   (C) Meeting friends.   (D) Meeting the principal.

_____ 3. Why did Bob climb into the principal's office?

(A) Because its door was open.

(B) Because the school gates were closed.

(C) Because the room was full of people.

(D) Because the room was brilliantly lighted up.

_____ 4. What does "There is not a soul in here" in the last paragraph mean?

(A) The room was haunted.

(B) The room was very dark.

(C) There was no one in the room.

(D) It's cold in the room.

_____ 5. What is the humorous point of this story?

(A) The principal thought the chair could speak.

(B) The principal didn't know Bob was in his office.

(C) The principal himself didn't know the door was closed.

(D) The principal knew Bob was in his office and spoke in a casual way.

Try it! Fill in each blank with the correct word. Make changes if necessary.

allow	downtown	lead to	familiar	at last

1. The road _____ the train station.

2. This picture looks _____ . I have seen it before.

3. Since my sister wants to do some shopping, I will go _____ with her.

4. Andy studied hard and passed the exam _____ .

5. No one is _____ to eat in the MRT station.

Unit 16 Signs Speak Louder Than Words

You speak and write in words. The messages are then sent and received. People have been using words to communicate for so long. But what about communicating without the use of words?

Wear a smile, and you tell people you are in a good mood. You cry, and others know you feel down. If you raise your hand, the teacher gives you a chance to speak up or ask a question. In some cultures, you shake your head to say no and you nod to agree.

These are not the only things that carry messages. Signs may speak louder than words. For example, when the traffic lights turn red, car drivers have to stop, or a police officer may ask them to pull over. A sign on the wall may have smokers put out their cigarettes or else they will be fined. Maybe it's the first time you have realized that these signs speak to you. Anything else?

Artists paint to show their love for the evening sunshine. People draw to show their anger at wars and the bittersweetness of love. And the list goes on.

Reading Comprehension: Choose the best answer for each question.

_____ 1. The article is mainly about _____ .
   (A) what signs are used for
   (B) how people communicate by gestures
   (C) how people use words to express themselves
   (D) how people show their ideas or feelings without words

_____ 2. Which of the following can be used by people to communicate?
   (A) Words.   (B) Body language.
   (C) Facial expressions.   (D) All of the above.

_____ 3. A person raises the hand to show he or she _____.

(A) is in a good mood (B) feels down

(C) has a question to ask (D) agrees

_____ 4. When seeing traffic lights turn red, a car driver may _____.

(A) pull over (B) speed up (C) pick up speed (D) stop

_____ 5. Which of the following is NOT an example of "communicating without words?"

(A) A painting. (C) Music.

(C) A book. (D) All of the above.

Try it! Fill in each blank with the correct word. Make changes if necessary.

| put out | message | communicate | pull over | in a good mood |

1. Mary is not available now. Would you like to leave a _____?

2. Paul wears a big smile. It seems that he is _____.

3. Before leaving, don't forget to _____ the campfire.

4. The police officer asked the driver to _____ and gave him a ticket for speeding.

5. I usually _____ with my friends in the U.K. by e-mail.

Unit 17 The MBTI Fad in South Korea

The Myers-Briggs Type Indicator (MBTI) is a test about personalities made in 1943. It looks at four things: if you're more outgoing or quiet, if you focus on facts or possibilities, if you make decisions with your head or your heart, and if you like making plans or doing things on the spot. The test puts you into one of 16 personality groups.

In South Korea, many people really like the MBTI. They think it can help them find a suitable job or partner. Businesses use it to choose who to hire and team up at work. Even some dating apps use it to match people. But a number of critics say the MBTI isn't reliable. They think it cannot accurately measure people's personalities. They also worry that using it in the workplace can be unfair. For example, bosses might pick outgoing people over quiet ones, even if the quiet ones are better at the job.

Even with these problems, lots of people in South Korea still like the MBTI. Some even use it to guess the future. In a 2018 TV series, the MBTI was used to find criminals. The idea was that certain personality types were more likely to do certain crimes. But experts said this was a bad idea. They argued that things like how you grow up and where you live are more important than your personality in predicting if you'll commit a crime.

The TV series got canceled after one season because not many people watched it. But the fact that it was made at all shows how much the MBTI affects Korean society. Whether that's good or bad is still open to debate.

Reading Comprehension: Choose the best answer for each question.

_____ 1. What is the main purpose of the passage?

    (A) To promote the use of the MBTI in workplaces.

    (B) To criticize South Korean dating apps.

    (C) To discuss the unreliability of the MBTI.

(D) To support the cancellation of an unpopular TV series.

_____ 2. How is the passage organized?

(A) Chronologically.

(B) By listing advantages and disadvantages.

(C) By cause and effect.

(D) By comparing different personality tests.

_____ 3. What is the primary reason why businesses in South Korea use the MBTI?

(A) To determine who to hire and team up at work.

(B) To match employees with suitable partners.

(C) To predict future job performance.

(D) To criticize the hiring process.

_____ 4. Where is the most likely place to find information about the MBTI's impact on South Korean society?

(A) In a TV show script.

(B) In a history book about personality tests.

(C) In a guidebook for tourists in South Korea.

(D) In a South Korean newspaper article.

_____ 5. How does the author feel about the MBTI's influence on South Korean society?

(A) Enthusiastic.　　(B) Neutral.　　　(C) Critical.　　　(D) Confused.

☀Try it!　Fill in each blank with the correct word. Make changes if necessary.

| outgoing | measure | suitable | predict | reliable |

1. Mandy is very _____ , always talking and laughing with everyone.

2. Wearing warm clothes in winter is _____ to stay comfortable in the cold.

3. Some people believe they can _____ the weather by looking at the clouds.

4. Scientists use special tools to _____ the weight of objects.

5. A good friend is someone you can always count on; they are _____ .

Unit 18 Mind Your Mind!

Once upon a time, in a small, remote village, there was located the House of 1,000 Mirrors. One day, a happy dog came visiting this place. He climbed the stairs with a spring in his step. At the entrance, he first checked out the inside with great enthusiasm. To his amazement, he found another 1,000 happy dogs gazing at him. What's more, when he smiled, they smiled back at him. When leaving the House, he was satisfied and thought he should come here more often.

Later, a **blue** dog went to the same place, but it was a whole different story. Unlike the happy one, he dragged himself up the stairs as though he had something on his mind. As he looked inside, he saw 1,000 fierce dogs. He started barking at them angrily, only to find himself in terror, because all the other dogs growled back at him. When he left, he told himself not to ever come back to such a terrible place again.

What we learn from this story is—the way people look varies with our states of mind. So which kind of face do you want to see? It's totally up to you.

Reading Comprehension: Choose the best answer for each question.

_____ 1. The main idea of the story is that _____.

    (A) a happy dog has more company

    (B) one should stay calm in the face of danger

    (C) if a dog barks at other dogs, they will growl back at it.

    (D) our states of mind affect the way we perceive people or things around

_____ 2. Why did the happy dog find another 1,000 dogs smiling back at him?

    (A) Because he came visiting them a lot.

    (B) Because it was the way they greeted their guests.

    (C) Because he saw his own reflections in the mirrors.

    (D) Because he checked out the house with great enthusiasm.

_____ 3. Which of the following is NOT used to describe the blue dog?

     (A) Fierce.   (B) Happy.   (C) Angry.   (D) Lost in thought.

_____ 4. The word "blue" in paragraph 2 means _____ .

     (A) sad   (B) angry   (C) joyful   (D) pleased

_____ 5. In the story, the writer compares our states of mind to _____ .

     (A) dogs   (B) mirrors

     (C) a house   (D) a small, remote village

Try it! Fill in each blank with the correct word. Make changes if necessary.

once upon a time	locate	check out	enthusiasm	terror

1. _____ the list to see if you have missed anyone.

2. The little girl was so frightened that she screamed in _____ .

3. _____ , in a castle lived a prince and a princess.

4. Terry practices basketball with great _____ . He wants to be a professional player.

5. This tower is _____ on the top of the hill.

Unit 19　An Animated Career

As a child, Hayao Miyazaki had loved reading and drawing. After finishing college in 1963, Miyazaki started working at the Toei Animation Company. In 1984, *Nausicaä of the Valley of the Wind* hit the **big screen** in Japan. It is adapted from a comic book Miyazaki drawn. The film was a huge success, which helped bring Miyazaki's own animation company, Studio Ghibli, into being.

My Neighbor Totoro (1988) is one of Miyazaki's most popular movies. Children and young adults love it. It is a heart-warming story about the friendship between two sisters and a cat named "Totoro." The "Cat Bus," a cat that turns into a bus, and soot sprites, dust creatures that live in the dark, are interesting and lovable. *Spirited Away*, which came out in 2001, enjoyed even wider popularity than *My Neighbor Totoro*.

Creativity is what makes Miyazaki's movies special. A kingdom in the clouds or a moving castle captures people's imagination. A hint of magic adds color to these creative stories, too. People under a spell turn into pigs, birds, dragons, and so on. With an interesting plot and diverse characters, it is appropriate to say that Miyazaki's films are here to stay.

Reading Comprehension: Choose the best answer for each question.

_____ 1. The article is mainly about _____ .
　(A) Miyazaki's life　　　　　　　　(B) Miyazaki's childhood
　(C) the success of Miyazaki's works　(D) the magic in Miyazaki's movies

_____ 2. Miyazaki graduated from college in _____ .
　(A) 1936　　　　　(B) 1948　　　　　(C) 1963　　　　　(D) 1984

_____ 3. After _____ came out, Miyazaki set up his own animation company.

　　(A) *Princess Mononoke*

　　(B) *My Neighbor Totoro*

　　(C) *Spirited Away*

　　(D) *Nausicaä of the Valley of the Wind*

_____ 4. The phrase "big screen" in the first paragraph means _____.

　　(A) the cinema

　　(B) the flat surface at the front of a television

　　(C) a wire or plastic net used to keep out insects

　　(D) something that prevents someone from seeing

_____ 5. Which of the following is true?

　　(A) A hint of magic is what makes Miyazaki's movies special.

　　(B) *Spirited Away* is even more successful than *My Neighbor Totoro*.

　　(C) *My Neighbor Totoro* talks about the friendship between two sisters and soot sprites.

　　(D) *Nausicaä of the Valley of the Wind* is adapted from a comic book drawn by two sisters.

Try it!　Fill in each blank with the correct word. Make changes if necessary.

friendship	come out	capture	imagination	creative

1. The teacher asked the students to use their _____ and tell her what the stone looked like.

2. The painter is very _____; she often has new ideas for her works.

3. The writer's new book will _____ next month.

4. My _____ with Lillian began in college, and we are still close friends now.

5. The worker's diligence _____ the foreman's attention.

Unit 20   The Power of Love

There may be a new **twist** to the meaning of "Love conquers all." The following is a true story between a mother and a child, which happened in the Australian Outback.

One day, a single mom named Liz was doing the laundry while her 5-year-old son, Eric, was playing in the backyard alone.

Suddenly, Liz heard a cry from the backyard. She rushed out of the back door and found a big snake was about to eat her son up! That scared Liz. But, then and there, she decided to get her son back to safety. Totally unaware of how dangerous the situation was, Liz grabbed a hoe and hit the monster hard.

Frantically, Liz hit the snake again and again. However, Eric's breath only grew weaker and Liz went nearly mad — she threw herself at the snake, opened her mouth and bit into its body.

On seeing the wound she bit on the monster, Liz picked up the hoe again and hit the wound with all her strength. The snake was so badly wounded that it had to let go of the boy to run away. It never occurred to the monster that a human's bite could do so much harm! It was a mother's love that turned things around.

Reading Comprehension: Choose the best answer for each question.

_____ 1. The article is mainly about _____ .
   (A) how great a mother's love is
   (B) how dangerous snakes may be
   (C) how much harm a human's bite can do
   (D) what humans can do in case of emergency

_____ 2. What does the word "twist" in the first paragraph mean?

(A) A sharp turn in a road.

(B) A change of meaning.

(C) An unexpected guest.

(D) The action of turning something with hands.

_____ 3. What happened while Eric was playing in the backyard?

(A) He tried to bite a snake.

(B) He was attacked by a snake.

(C) A snake tried to eat up his mother.

(D) He grabbed a hoe and hit a snake hard.

_____ 4. Why did the snake let go of the boy?

(A) Because it was afraid of hoes.

(B) Because it was seriously hurt.

(C) Because it was bitten by the boy.

(D) Because its breath grew weaker and weaker.

_____ 5. Which of the following is true?

(A) The boy didn't live with his father.

(B) Liz bit the snake because she was out of her mind.

(C) The saying "Love conquers all" cannot be applied to the story.

(D) Liz wounded the snake with a gun first and then bit it with all her strength.

Try it!　Fill in each blank with the correct word. Make changes if necessary.

| conquer | eat up | scare | then and there | grab |

1. The old woman was _____ by the sight of the dead man.

2. Mark cannot _____ his fear of flying, so he never travels by plane.

3. Betty saw her boyfriend dating another girl; she decided _____ to break up with him.

4. The policeman _____ the thief by the arm.

5. The boy _____ all the food; he left nothing for his sister to eat.

Unit 21 　Where Chewing Gum Began

The history of chewing gum has been for a long time. Swedish scientists discovered a piece of gum that can be traced back to 9,000 years ago. On this gum, the marks of a teenager's teeth are even visible! However, modern gum didn't exist until around 1870. Wanting to make rubber in the first place, Thomas Adams got some liquid from a tree in Mexico, and he ended up finding how to produce chewing gum. Later, his gum became a **hit**, and more and more people started going into the gum business.

1892 marked the year William Wrigley started his gum business. His gum became popular with Americans, and he made a fortune out of it. Nowadays, the Wrigley Company's gum production level reaches one billion sticks a year. Every year, 170 to 180 pieces of gum is consumed per person in the U.S.

However, some don't welcome the situation, including those working at the Statue of Liberty. They had so much gum to clean that a trash can was put in place. Over the can was a sign reading: "Put your gum here." But people just took it literally—they actually stuck their gum on the sign!

Reading Comprehension: Choose the best answer for each question.

_____ 1. The article is mainly about _____.
    (A) the history of chewing gum
    (B) the production of chewing gum
    (C) the business of chewing gum
    (D) the inventor of chewing gum

_____ 2. Modern gum can be traced back to about _____ years ago.
    (A) 140   (B) 180   (C) 1,870   (D) 9,000

_____ 3. Who invented chewing gum?
    (A) A Mexican.   (B) Thomas Adams.
    (C) William Wrigley.   (D) Swedish scientists.

_____ 4. In _____ , William Wrigley started his gum business.

     (A) 1870   (B) 1829   (C) 1892   (D) 1982

_____ 5. Which of the following is true?

     (A) The word "hit" in the first paragraph means failure.

     (B) William Wrigley made a fortune in rubber production.

     (C) In the States, a person consumes 170 to 180 pieces of gum a year, on average.

     (D) At the Statue of Liberty, people were asked to stick their chewing gum onto a sign over a trash can.

Try it! Fill in each blank with the correct word. Make changes if necessary.

production	discover	trace back	make a fortune	consume

1. "Who was the first person to _____ America?" "Christopher Columbus."

2. To lose weight, you must stop _____ fast food.

3. The businessman has _____ in the tourist trade.

4. A drop in oil _____ results in a rise in its price.

5. The tradition of kite-flying can be _____ to centuries ago.

Unit 22　The American Character

For many people, expressions like "Get to the point," "Speak your mind," or "Just do it" are so American. The direct American style **stands up for** what is right, yet it might surprise people from other parts of the world.

For example, American children are not afraid of questioning their parents and teachers about their ideas. Office workers are encouraged to speak up in front of the manager. However, a respect for the elderly and those in power is very important in some cultures. They prefer using hints to express themselves so as to avoid hurting others' feelings.

Another feature of American style is competition. It drives people to "think big," to "make it happen," and be the "A players." But, Americans may come across as pushy or not easy to work along with.

Americans like what is fast and workable. They like the no-nonsense type of guys who waste no time. But recently Europe has seen the rise of the Slow Movement. There is a rethinking of doing things the old ways.

Though it is impossible to work out each of the differences, most foreigners still find Americans friendly, lively, and creative. That is why people around the world have come to America to look for a new life and chances.

Reading Comprehension: Choose the best answer for each question.

_____ 1. The article is mainly about _____ .

    (A) American spirit

    (B) American customs

    (C) common expressions used by Americans

    (D) American children's attitude problem

_____ 2. The phrase "stand up for" in the first paragraph means _____.

    (A) being easily seen   (B) resisting someone

    (C) being on one's feet   (D) supporting something

_____ 3. People use hints for fear of _____.

    (A) thinking big   (B) being the A player

    (C) expressing themselves   (D) hurting others' feelings

_____ 4. Which of the following is a feature of American style?

    (A) Competition.   (B) Being direct.

    (C) Being fast and workable.   (D) All of the above.

_____ 5. Which of the following is true?

    (A) Recently, the U.S. has seen the rise of the Slow Movement.

    (B) The expression "Get to the point" shows that Americans like to be direct.

    (C) Competition makes Americans easy to get along with.

    (D) Most foreigners find Americans friendly after working out the differences between them.

Try it!   Fill in each blank with the correct word. Make changes if necessary.

direct	speak up	hint	feature	competition

1. There is fierce _____ among the candidates; everyone wants to get the job.

2. You may _____ in the meeting. Any opinion is welcomed.

3. Each tea pot in this tea shop has its own distinctive _____.

4. Don't beat around the bush. Just give me a _____ answer.

5. Lily gave her friend a pinch at the arm, dropping a _____ that she didn't want to talk about her boyfriend in front of her parents.

Unit 23 Travel Your Way

Modern life without traveling is unimaginable. The fastest way to travel is by plane. Today, you may book flights and enjoy a one-day trip, which used to take more than a month to complete a century ago.

Traveling by train takes longer, but it has its own advantages. You can take a closer look at the country you are traveling through. Modern trains offer comfortable seats and dining areas. Even the longest journey can make you feel short.

Some prefer traveling by sea. Ocean liners have been around for a long time. They often feature five-star lodging and nice food. Besides, you'll never be bored with so many exciting activities on deck.

Others like to travel by car. You can go in the way of your own schedule and plan. For example, you're free to travel 2 miles a day, or 50 to as long as 200 miles. And stop wherever you want, like at the woods for some fresh air, at a beach for a swim, or at a hotel for some rest. That is why more people drive to enjoy their trips, while business people opt for the train or airplane since they have little time on their hands.

Reading Comprehension: Choose the best answer for each question.

_____ 1. The article is mainly about _____.
   (A) traveling   (B) modern life
   (C) modern trains   (D) ocean liners

_____ 2. If you are a businessman who has little time, you may travel by _____.
   (A) train   (B) bike   (C) plane   (D) ocean liner

_____ 3. What is the advantage of traveling by train?

    (A) You may save a lot of time.

    (B) You may stop wherever you want.

    (C) You may enjoy many exciting activities on deck.

    (D) You can take a closer look at the place where you are traveling.

_____ 4. What is the advantage of traveling by car?

    (A) It is the fastest way to travel.

    (B) You may get comfortable seats and dining areas.

    (C) You may get five-star lodging and nice food.

    (D) You can travel according to your plan and schedule.

_____ 5. Which of the following is true?

    (A) Modern trains feature five-star lodging and nice food.

    (B) Traveling by train takes longer, and it has no advantages at all.

    (C) A one-day trip today may take a month or more to complete in the past.

    (D) With comfortable seats and dining areas, the longest journey by plane can make people feel short.

Try it! Fill in each blank with the correct word. Make changes if necessary.

used to	complete	advantage	journey	opt for

1. Sabrina will _____ her report tonight since the deadline is tomorrow.

2. Marco Polo wrote a book describing his _____ through China.

3. Julie _____ a two-day trip to Kenting rather than a whole weekend of staying home.

4. I _____ go jogging in the morning. Now, since I have to arrive at the office earlier, I don't jog now.

5. One of the _____ of taking exercise is helping you keep fit.

Unit 24 Where Did Noodles Come From?

Noodles are popular in many countries around the world, but for many years, people have debated about exactly where they were invented. Some say that the Italians invented noodles and brought them to China along the Silk Road. Others say that the Arabs invented noodles and then shared them with Italy and China. And many Chinese claim that noodles were invented in China and then spread to the Middle East, Italy, and the rest of the world via the Silk Road.

A recent discovery in China, however, may settle this debate once and for all. The earliest noodles in the world have been found in an archaeological site near the Yellow River. These noodles are more than 4,000 years old. Unlike modern noodles made from wheat flour, however, they were made from millet. Yellow in color, the noodles were found in a pot that had been buried in a major flood. According to one scientist at the site, they looked like "Ramen," or traditional Chinese "pulled" noodles.

So, with the discovery of the world's earliest noodles in China, it seems safe to say that noodles were invented there, and they later spread to the rest of the world by way of the Silk Road.

Reading Comprehension: Choose the best answer for each question.

_____ 1. Many people said they invented noodles except _____ .

    (A) the Chinese   (B) the Arabs   (C) the Italians   (D) the Spanish

_____ 2. Noodles were spread to other countries through _____ .

    (A) the Yellow River   (B) the Silk Road

    (C) the Great Wall   (D) the Arabian Sea

_____ 3. The purpose of the article is _____ .

　　(A) to suggest that noodles are the best food in the world

　　(B) to ensure that China plays a role in the art of cooking noodles

　　(C) to explain where noodles were invented

　　(D) to discuss why noodles are popular in many places

_____ 4. Modern noodles are made from _____ .

　　(A) millet　　　　(B) brown rice　　(C) wheat flour　　(D) corn

_____ 5. About the earliest noodles, which statement is true?

　　(A) They were found near the Yellow River.

　　(B) They were more than 40,000 years old.

　　(C) They were found in a pot in the mountains.

　　(D) They looked like traditional Japanese "pulled" noodles.

Try it! Fill in each blank with the correct word. Make changes if necessary.

debate	claim	wheat	bury	according to

1. _____ the news report, a plane crashed into the sea yesterday.

2. Linda is health-conscious; she prefers whole _____ bread to white bread.

3. The dog _____ its bone somewhere in the park.

4. The man _____ that he has never stolen anyone's money.

5. A meeting will be held tomorrow to _____ how the money should be used to save the poor.

Unit 25 Let's Go Camping!

Nowadays, camping is more popular than ever. In the UK, for example, the number of people who go camping has gone up by 20% in the last two years. However, the camping craze is not just in the UK. It's common to see people with tents and campfires in parks, forests, and mountains across various countries.

So why is camping so popular? One of the reasons is that it's a cheap holiday option. You don't need to spend a lot of money on a hotel, and you can cook your own food. So it's perfect if you're trying to save money. Another reason is that it helps you get away from technology. These days, we're always on our phones, but when you're camping, you can switch off all your smartphones and enjoy the simple things in life.

But what if you don't like the idea of sleeping in a tent? Well, now there's a new camping trend called "glamping." Glamping is where you stay in a luxury tent with a real bed, a fridge, and even a TV! It's basically like staying in a hotel, but in the great outdoors. There are glamping sites all over the world, including some beautiful ones in Africa, Asia, and South America. So if you want to try camping but you don't want to give up your home comforts, maybe glamping is for you.

Of course, camping isn't for everyone. Some people hate the idea of sleeping outside, and others think it's boring because there's nothing to do. But if you've never been camping before, maybe it's time to give it a go. You might just discover a new hobby and join the camping craze!

Reading Comprehension: Choose the best answer for each question.

_____ 1. What is the purpose of this passage?

    (A) To persuade people not to try camping.

    (B) To promote the benefits of glamping.

(C) To discuss the popularity of camping.

(D) To comparing camping to other outdoor activities.

_____ 2. How does the author begin the passage?

(A) By telling a joke.　　　　　(B) By giving a definition.

(C) By mentioning a story.　　　(D) By providing statistics.

_____ 3. According to the passage, why has camping become more popular?

(A) Camping becomes an expensive holiday option.

(B) Camping allows people to disconnect from technology.

(C) Camping offers a lot of hotel options.

(D) Camping outdoors is more comfortable than staying in hotels.

_____ 4. Which of the following is NOT mentioned as a reason why some people dislike camping?

(A) They prefer to sleep indoors.

(B) They find camping boring.

(C) They are unable to afford camping equipment.

(D) They think camping offers fewer activities.

_____ 5. According to the passage, which of the following is true about glamping?

(A) It refers to camping in bad weather conditions.

(B) It means camping without any technological devices.

(C) It refers to staying in a luxury tent with home comforts.

(D) It means traditional camping with basic facilities.

Try it! Fill in each blank with the correct word. Make changes if necessary.

option	tent	comfort	give up	switch off

1. Lynn prefers the hotel which offers home _____ .
2. My father put up a small _____ in the campground.
3. Remember to _____ the lights before leaving the house.
4. Don't _____ learning new things; otherwise, you'll miss out on valuable opportunities for personal growth.
5. Having a picnic is a great _____ for a relaxing weekend activity.

Unit 26　Fire! Escape!

Every year, fires take away thousands of lives. A fire often starts without warning. People who die in a fire are usually too scared to react when it breaks out. Here are some tips that will help you through an emergency.

· Upon smelling smoke or seeing the fire, shout "Fire!" as loudly as you can. Do so because your family or neighbors may be asleep.

· However small a fire is, never try to put it out yourself. Ask people for help or dial 911. Tell the fire department workers your location and what is on fire. Stay calm and do as you're told.

· If your room is full of smoke, keep your body low. Less smoke near the floor means more fresh air and better chances to see where you are going.

· Test the doorknob before you open a door. Try it with the back of your hand. If it is cool, open the door carefully. If it is hot, you'll need to try a different way out.

· One last reminder: Get out of your house as soon as a fire starts. Never stop to pick up anything. The fire grows more quickly than you can imagine.

Reading Comprehension: Choose the best answer for each question.

_____ 1. The article is mainly about _____.
　　(A) how fast a fire may grow
　　(B) tips on how to put out a fire by yourself
　　(C) how to find a way out of a burning house
　　(D) tips on how to keep oneself safe in a fire

_____ 2. What should a person do when seeing a fire or smelling smoke?
　　(A) Shout "Fire!"　　　　　　(B) Call 911.
　　(C) Stay calm.　　　　　　　(D) All of the above.

_____ 3. When finding a way out of a burning house, one should _____.

(A) test the doorknob after opening a door

(B) touch the doorknob carefully before opening a door

(C) pick up all the personal belongings before leaving

(D) hold the doorknob in his or her hand tight before opening a door

_____ 4. People should keep their bodies low when the room is full of smoke because _____.

(A) doorknobs are hot

(B) there is more smoke near the floor

(C) there is less fresh air near the floor

(D) they may be able to see where they are going

_____ 5. Why should a person get out of a burning house as soon as possible?

(A) Because doorknobs will turn very hot.

(B) Because the fire may spread very quickly.

(C) Because he or she is usually too scared to react.

(D) Because his or her family and neighbors may be asleep.

Try it! Fill in each blank with the correct word. Make changes if necessary.

imagine	emergency	location	be full of	as soon as

1. Call 911 in case of _____.

2. Every Friday night, the movie theater _____ people.

3. The little girl likes to _____ herself as a beautiful princess.

4. The dog barked at me _____ it saw me.

5. This hotel is very popular because its _____ is close to the train station.

Unit 27　A Victorious Plant

Near the end of the 1st century A.D., wars broke out between the Romans and the Scots. After **capturing** England, the Romans tried to gain control over Scotland. A strong Roman army was then sent north and each solider was burning to kill.

The Scots seemed to be **fighting a losing battle** because there were simply too many Roman soldiers. The night before the final battle, the Scottish general spoke to his men.

"Tomorrow, we're in for a battle that could make or break us," said the general, "Rest now and we are to fight till the end!" The soldiers roared.

Under the cover of darkness, the Romans secretly made their way up the hill. The surprise attack could begin in any minute.

Suddenly, a cry from among the Romans broke the silence. It came from a soldier who hurt his foot on a thistle. Alarmed, the Scots got on their feet and fought like there was no tomorrow. They beat the Romans in no time.

The thistle had been largely unknown to people. They grow in the wild and are covered in sharp points. Few people like it, yet the Scottish love it, so much that they named it their national flower.

Reading Comprehension: Choose the best answer for each question.

_____ 1. The article is mainly about _____.

    (A) the national flag of Scotland

    (B) the national flower of Scotland

    (C) the fall of England in the 1st century A.D.

    (D) a battle between the Scots and the Romans in the 1st century A.D.

_____ 2. The word "capture" in the first paragraph means _____.

    (A) catching a person or an animal

    (B) taking control of a place

    (C) making someone interested in something

    (D) filming or recording someone or something

_____ 3. Why did the Scots seem to be fighting a losing battle?

    (A) Because the Romans had captured England.

    (B) Because there were too many Roman soldiers.

    (C) Because the Roman soldiers were burning to kill.

    (D) Because the night fell before the final battle broke out.

_____ 4. Why did the Scottish love the thistle?

    (A) Because it grows in the wild.

    (B) Because it is covered with sharp points.

    (C) Because it was largely unknown to people.

    (D) Because it helped them win the battle against the Romans.

_____ 5. Which of the following is true?

    (A) To capture Scotland, a strong Roman army was sent south.

    (B) Morale among the Scottish soldiers was low before the battle.

    (C) The Romans tried to capture England after they gained control over Scotland.

    (D) "Fighting a losing battle" means doing something that will probably make someone succeed.

Try it!   Fill in each blank with the correct word. Make changes if necessary.

break out	battle	attack	silence	alarm

1. The general died in a bloody _____ in World War I.

2. _____ by the bad news, Lisa was worried about her son.

3. The war _____, and many soldiers fought bravely.

4. The army launched a surprise _____ on their enemy.

5. The roar of a thunderclap broke the _____ of the night.

Unit 28 The Antidepressant in the Great Depression

When the New York stock market crashed in 1929, a period of economic decline began. This period is rightly called the Great Depression. It lasted 10 years, and millions of people lost their jobs and homes. Yet, not everything from the Depression was bad. There was still some light in the darkness. In 1935, U.S. President, Franklin D. Roosevelt established the Works Progress Administration (WPA), which tried to create jobs and make the economy better. It helped people from all walks of life.

One part of the WPA program—the Federal Writers' Project (FWP)—was especially helpful to jobless writers. In as short as eight years, the FWP handed out jobs to numerous writers. Among them were Saul Bellow and Richard Wright, both of whom later became famous authors.

The project, though, is famous for the guides it produced. The FWP created guides for 48 states of the U.S., helping people know about cities and cultures. The project also included a discussion on ethnic groups. Thus, it produced studies like *The Italians of New York*, and 2,000 former slaves were interviewed. The FWP tried to **boost** Americans' spirits during the Depression by allowing them to understand each other and creating a sense of national unity. Indeed, not everything was depressing during the Great Depression.

Reading Comprehension: Choose the best answer for each question.

_____ 1. The Great Depression lasted from _____.

　　(A) 1935 to 1939　(B) 1929 to 1935　(C) 1929 to 1939　(D) 1938 to 1948

_____ 2. Which of the following statements about the WPA is NOT true?

(A) It was established by President Franklin D. Roosevelt.

(B) It tried to create jobs and make the economy better.

(C) It helped writers who didn't have jobs.

(D) It had 6,600 employees.

_____ 3. What does the word "boost" mean in the last paragraph?

(A) To talk about something proudly.

(B) To raise something to a higher position.

(C) To move something to a lower level.

(D) To travel to some other places.

_____ 4. Which of the following statements about the Great Depression is NOT true?

(A) The economy collapsed and everything was depressing.

(B) Many people lost jobs and homes.

(C) It began when the New York stock market crashed.

(D) President Roosevelt tried to make the economy better during this period.

_____ 5. The FWP tried to _____ during the Great Depression.

(A) help people know their cities and understand each other

(B) hire writers to produce some travel guidebooks

(C) make books about the economic problems the country met

(D) record how hard people's lives were

Try it! Fill in each blank with the correct word. Make changes if necessary.

crash	a walk of life	project	interview	unity

1. The characters in the play include people from all _____ .

2. He became poor because of the big stock market _____ .

3. The scientist has worked on the _____ for a month but is still getting nowhere.

4. It's difficult for a country to reach political _____ .

5. The new president was _____ on television yesterday.

Unit 29　More Than an Image on a Bill

There are many famous inventors from the U.S. However, Benjamin Franklin is probably one of the most famous American ones. Although he was also a writer and a philosopher, Franklin is best remembered today for his many inventions.

Franklin invented a lot of useful things mostly because he needed them. For example, Franklin wore glasses, but as he got older, he needed another pair to read. Getting tired of changing between two pairs of glasses, Franklin decided to invent one pair that would help him see clearly both things near and far. These glasses are now known as bifocals. Franklin also invented a special iron stove, the Franklin stove. It allowed people to heat their homes less dangerously and with less wood than traditional fireplaces did.

Moreover, you may have heard the story of Franklin's famous kite flight, but it is not true that Franklin discovered electricity. Franklin just proved that lightning is a form of electricity. However, from this experience, Franklin gained the knowledge to invent the lightning rod, which is a device that protects buildings and ships from lightning.

Without a doubt, Benjamin Franklin invented many useful things. Though he accomplished many things in politics, wrote several famous books, and his image was even put on the U.S. hundred-dollar bill, Franklin remains best known for his countless inventions.

Reading Comprehension: Choose the best answer for each question.

_____ 1. The article is mainly about _____ .

(A) famous inventors around the world

(B) Franklin and his inventions

(C) Franklin as a writer

(D) how reading glasses are made

_____ 2. According to the article, who discovered electricity?

(A) The kite.   (B) Benjamin Franklin.

(C) An American philosopher.   (D) We can't infer this from the article.

_____ 3. Franklin invented things usually because _____ .

(A) he would like to be remembered   (B) he wanted to use less wood

(C) he was in need of them   (D) he had no money

_____ 4. According to the article, the lightning rod _____ .

(A) looks like a kite   (B) helps people heat their homes

(C) can protect ships from lightning   (D) is not used anymore now

_____ 5. Which of the following can also be the title of this article?

(A) How to Become a Famous Inventor

(B) The Most Famous U.S. Inventor

(C) Benjamin Franklin and His Glasses

(D) The Importance of Benjamin Franklin's Inventions

Try it! Fill in each blank with the correct word. Make changes if necessary.

inventor	famous	device	lightning	image

1. The singer's _____ was printed on the T-shirt.

2. This city is _____ for its exquisite architecture.

3. It's going to rain soon because I just saw _____ flash.

4. This useful _____ makes it easy for you to cut grass.

5. Thomas Edison is a great American _____ .

Unit 30 Hope

by Emily Dickinson

Hope is the thing with feathers

That perches in the soul,

And sings the tune—without the words,

And never stops at all,

And sweetest in the gale is heard;

And sore must be the storm

That could abash the little bird

That kept so many warm.

I've heard it in the chilliest land,

And on the strangest sea;

Yet, never, in extremity,

It asked a crumb of me.

Reading Comprehension: Choose the best answer for each question.

_____ 1. In the first stanza, why does the poet say hope sings the tune and never stops at all?

(A) Because hope keeps giving people strength to face problems.

(B) Because hope makes people stay in tune.

(C) Because if people have hope, they can sing well.

(D) Because people who never stop singing will succeed.

_____ 2. The poet compares hope to a _____ .

(A) feather   (B) breeze   (C) gale   (D) bird

_____ 3. In the last stanza, the chilliest land and the strangest sea refer to places that
are _____ to live in.

(A) cold   (B) easy   (C) poor   (D) difficult

_____ 4. From the last two lines we learn that _____ .

(A) hope is the reward when the time is tough

(B) hope never expects anything in return

(C) hope is the last thing we should give up

(D) life goes on even if there is little hope left

_____ 5. The overall tone of this poem is _____ .

(A) negative   (B) changing   (C) weak   (D) encouraging

Try it! Fill in each blank with the correct word. Make changes if necessary.

| feather | soul | tune | chilly | ask of |

1. It is normally very _____ at this time of the year here.

2. The criminal's _____ is seized by the Devil. He can't help repeating
the same mistakes.

3. The _____ the composer wrote is really pleasing.

4. Ducks' _____ are waterproof so they can swim on the water.

5. Can I _____ a favor _____ you?

Unit 31 Beyond Words

As a student of English, you may have already known it is not smart to translate a sentence word for word. Take the sentence "How's it going?" Look up each of the words, put all the meanings together in your mother **tongue** and what do you get? Chances are you will have something that sounds like nonsense.

Typically, students of English are first told to work on word meanings. Yet, communication is never just about putting words together. You'll need to put them in the right order. That's when rules of word order come into play. If a speaker gets the order wrong, people will have a hard time understanding each other. Oftentimes, when the order of words is changed, so is the meaning of the sentence. For example, "She only reads *Newsweek*" is different from "Only she reads *Newsweek*." Sometimes a change in word order doesn't change the meaning of the sentence, though. For example, "Wayne gave food to the beggar" is the same as "Wayne gave the beggar food."

Therefore, advanced learners have to go beyond the study of words. As they read more, they will be able to tell quickly which words go well together and which don't. Once you are very good at this, you'll sound pretty much like a native speaker.

Reading Comprehension: Choose the best answer for each question.

_____ 1. The article is mainly about _____ .
(A) how to master English
(B) how to change the order of words
(C) how to translate English into Chinese
(D) why to learn about rules of word order

_____ 2. The best way to translate an English sentence is _____.

    (A) translating it word for word   (B) looking up each of the words

    (C) changing the word order   (D) None of the above.

_____ 3. If you get word order of a sentence wrong, _____.

    (A) rules of word order come into play

    (B) people will have difficulty understanding you

    (C) the meaning of the sentence will remain the same

    (D) people will be able to tell quickly which words go well together

_____ 4. The word "tongue" in the first paragraph means _____.

    (A) a language   (B) a particular way of speaking

    (C) something long and narrow   (D) the soft part inside the mouth

_____ 5. Which of the following is true?

    (A) Communication is just about putting words together.

    (B) English students often translate a sentence word for word.

    (C) The usage "give something to someone" and "give someone something" mean the same.

    (D) If the word order is wrong, people still can understand each other.

Try it! Fill in each blank with the correct word. Make changes if necessary.

translate	look up	nonsense	work on	come into play

1. What the drunk said was _____. No one could understand him.

2. As the Internet _____, the way of communication among people has been changed greatly.

3. Wayne spent two months _____ the book from French into Chinese.

4. You may _____ the opening time of the department store online.

5. The scientist has been _____ the problem for months, but still has not found out the solution.

Unit 32 What's in a Name of a Storm?

A tropical cyclone is a storm that forms in the hottest part of the world, that is, in the tropics. The storm moves fast in a circle. It can bring winds reaching 60 kph or up. Such storms take different names in different parts of the world. In Asia Pacific, people have "typhoons" while storms that hit the Americas are called "hurricanes," as the famous Hurricane Katrina that struck southeastern United States in 2005.

The World Meteorological Organization (WMO) keeps a close watch on tropical cyclones and gives forecasts and warnings. It also makes lists of names for storms in A to Z order. If the first storm of the year gets the name Al, the next may be named Barbara. Names starting with the letters O, U, X, Y, and Z cannot be found on the list because fewer names start with these letters.

So, when a cyclone forms at sea, scientists pick a name for it. It can be a man's name or a woman's. However, in Asian countries, the name list is a little different. Names of animals and plants are more common than people's names. These names help the public catch up with the latest news on the storm.

Reading Comprehension: Choose the best answer for each question.

_____ 1. The article is mainly about _____ .
  (A) cyclones in Asia Pacific
  (B) the names of tropical cyclones
  (C) the destructiveness of tropical cyclones
  (D) the differences between typhoons and hurricanes

_____ 2. Name lists for tropical cyclones are put in order of _____ .
  (A) time   (B) number   (C) spelling   (D) importance

_____ 3. The name of a tropical cyclone can be _____.

    (A) a man's name   (B) a woman's name

    (C) an animal's name   (D) All of the above.

_____ 4. Which of the following might be a storm's name?

    (A) Oliver.   (B) York.

    (C) Zoe.   (D) Wendy.

_____ 5. Which of the following is true?

    (A) The tropics are the hottest part of the world.

    (B) In Asia Pacific, tropical cyclones are called hurricanes.

    (C) A tropical cyclone forms in the coldest part of the world.

    (D) In the Americas, cyclones are commonly named after plants and animals.

Try it! Fill in each blank with the correct word. Make changes if necessary.

| strike | catch up with | organization | forecast | warning |

1. According to the weather _____, it will be cold this afternoon.
2. An earthquake _____ the city yesterday and caused great damage.
3. The UN is an international _____ whose goal is to keep world peace.
4. The teacher gave Peter a _____ that she would punish him if he made the same mistake again.
5. Angel has missed many classes; she is trying hard to _____ her classmates.

Unit 33 Penguins in Danger

One of the most lovable bird species in nature—penguins—could be dying out. In fact, 10 of the 17 kinds of them could be gone altogether in the near future. The penguin population has **shrunk** 30% in the last decade or so. Before looking at the causes of this crisis, here are some quick facts about the birds.

Penguins are black and white birds that make their home in the southern half of the earth, such as Antarctica, New Zealand, and Australia. They live in cold waters and feed on fish and shrimp-like beings. Penguins cannot fly but they make wonderful swimmers.

Let's go back to the reasons behind the crisis. First of all, global warming spells trouble for penguins. This is because the sea animals penguins eat cannot survive in warmer waters. Penguins may end up dying due to a lack of food. Oil drilling and oil leaks, on the other hand, put penguins in danger. Lastly, sea lions or seals are always hunting penguins for food.

Though damage to penguins cannot be undone, it's a comfort to know that a lot of people are trying to help. A few years ago, an oil spill left 40% of the penguins in South Africa oil-covered. Happily, thousands of people offered to clean the birds. They cared for the birds until they got well and were freed back into the wild.

Reading Comprehension: Choose the best answer for each question.

_____ 1. The article mainly talks about _____.
  (A) why many people like penguins
  (B) how to save penguins from extinction
  (C) why penguins are in danger of extinction
  (D) why penguins can make wonderful swimmers

_____ 2. How many kinds of penguins will die out in the near future?

(A) 10.   (B) 17.   (C) 30.   (D) 40.

_____ 3. The word "shrink" in the first paragraph means _____.

(A) becoming greater in amount

(B) becoming smaller in amount

(C) moving back or away from something

(D) becoming smaller when washed in hot water

_____ 4. What leads penguins to extinction?

(A) Oil leaks.   (B) Oil drilling.

(C) Global warming.   (D) All of the above.

_____ 5. Which of the following is true?

(A) There are 17 kinds of penguins in the world.

(B) Penguins are black and white sea animals.

(C) Penguins make their home in the Northern hemisphere.

(D) Because of global warming, penguins may die out due to a lack of water.

Try it! Fill in each blank with the correct word. Make changes if necessary.

| die out | shrink | crisis | survive | end up |

1. Carl's relationship with his girlfriend was in _____; they might soon break up.

2. No one on the plane _____. All the passengers died in the crash.

3. We must protect pandas, or they will soon _____.

4. If Frank keeps smoking, he may _____ getting lung cancer.

5. The population of this town _____ because most young people moved into the cities.

Unit 34 International Dog Day

International Dog Day falls on August 26th each year. It's a special day to celebrate and thank dogs for the happiness and love they bring to us. On this day, people do different things to show their love for dogs. Here are some examples.

Adopt a dog	If you're thinking about getting a dog, this could be a great day to do it. Lots of dogs in shelters need homes, and adopting a dog can bring joy to both you and the dog.
Spend time with your dog	Take your dog for a walk, play in the park, or just cuddle on the couch. Dogs love attention, and spending time together makes your **bond** stronger.
Give treats	Make a special meal or prepare treats for your dog. You can also get them a new toy or a comfortable bed. Dogs appreciate these little things, and it makes them feel loved.
Help at a shelter	If you don't have a dog, spend time volunteering at an animal shelter. You can help take care of the dogs there by feeding, grooming, or playing with them.
Donate to dog charities	Support groups that work to keep dogs safe and happy. You can give money, food, toys, or other things. Every bit helps make life better for dogs.

Dogs are known as our best friends because they're loyal and loving. People have had dogs as friends for a very long time, and dogs have helped us with things like hunting and protecting us. Nowadays, many folks have dogs as pets and treat them like family. Dogs give us love every day, and International Dog Day is a chance to **give some love back**!

 Reading Comprehension: Choose the best answer for each question.

_____ 1. What is the main purpose of International Dog Day?

　　(A) To sell special dog treats.　　　(B) To celebrate and appreciate dogs.

　　(C) To promote dog adoption.　　　(D) To organize dog shows.

_____ 2. According to the passage, what is a suggested way to celebrate International Dog Day?

　　(A) Buy a new dog.　　　　　　　(B) Attend a dog show.

　　(C) Only donate to dog charities.　　(D) Spend time with your dog.

_____ 3. What does the word "bond" mean in the passage?

　　(A) A financial investment.　　　　(B) A connection or relationship.

　　(C) A type of dog breed.　　　　　(D) A form of dog treat.

_____ 4. Why do some people consider dogs as their best friends, according to the passage?

　　(A) Because dogs are great at hunting.

　　(B) Because dogs are good protectors.

　　(C) Because dogs are loyal and loving.

　　(D) Because dogs are easy to train.

_____ 5. What does the author imply by "give some love back" in the last paragraph?

　　(A) Repay your dog for their love and companionship.

　　(B) Give a portion of your love to strangers.

　　(C) Exchange love for material possessions.

　　(D) Reserve some love for future use.

Try it!　Fill in each blank with the correct word. Make changes if necessary.

cuddle	shelter	adopt	happiness	volunteer

1. Many families choose to _____ a pet from the local animal shelter.

2. The community organized a _____ for people affected by the storm.

3. Students _____ at the local community center to help others yesterday.

4. After a long day, it's nice to _____ with a cozy blanket.

5. Playing with friends brings joy and _____ to children.

Unit 35　Looking Into the Future

One day, Galileo got a letter from a friend in the Netherlands. "A man named Lippershey here made a special kind of glasses," the letter read, "I met him and asked him to show me the glasses. At that time, there seemed to be a beautiful lady far away. I looked at her through the glasses, and in that instant, I felt she was standing right in front of me. It was unbelievable! I thought she was within reach, so I reached for her but I fell over. Helping me **get to my feet**, Lippershey laughed because the lady was actually far away from us."

The letter gave Galileo some ideas. He decided to make a piece of glass of his own, or one that was even better. "With this piece of glass," Galileo thought, "not only will I see the lady, but I shall see the moon!" He soon began to work on his own piece of glass. He named it "telescope" ("tele" and "scope" mean "far" and "see" in Greek). When the work was done, Galileo used this piece of glass to look at the night sky. Words nearly failed him. The moon was almost right in front of him. While Lippershey could see across the land, Galileo could see across the sky.

Reading Comprehension: Choose the best answer for each question.

_____ 1. The article is mainly about _____ .

(A) the life of Galileo

(B) the invention of the telescope

(C) a letter from a friend of Galileo's

(D) the origin of the word "telescope"

_____ 2. Galileo is probably a _____ .

(A) a writer　　　(B) a doctor　　　(C) a teacher　　　(D) an astronomer

_____ 3. Why did Galileo's friend fall over?

(A) Because he couldn't stop laughing.

(B) Because Lippershey tripped him up.

(C) Because there was a woman standing in front of him.

(D) Because he tried to reach for a woman who was actually far away from him.

_____ 4. The phrase "get to one's feet" in the first paragraph means _____.

(A) standing up

(B) wearing shoes

(C) walking around

(D) making a great effort to do something

_____ 5. Which of the following is true?

(A) Galileo's friend was a Greek.

(B) In Greek, "scope" means "see."

(C) A man called Lippershey wrote to Galileo.

(D) Galileo's friend made a special kind of glasses.

Try it! Fill in each blank with the correct word. Make changes if necessary.

unbelievable	reach for	fall over	actually	of one's own

1. Since the road was muddy, some people _____.

2. Stella is _____ from the U.K., not the U.S.

3. Sandy smiled at her boyfriend and _____ his hand.

4. I don't want to share a room with my sister anymore. I want to have a room _____.

5. It is _____ that the team lost the game in the last 10 seconds.

Unit 36   Fukubukuro Lucky Bags

In Japan, there's something special called "Fukubukuro," also known as "lucky bags." These are bags filled with surprises and sold at a big discount during certain times. Each bag has a specific theme, such as beauty products or computer accessories. People in Japan enjoy these lucky bags as they provide a fun way to try your luck and make a good purchase.

Although nobody knows exactly who started selling the first Fukubukuro in Japan, there are some interesting stories about its origin. Some say it began in the Edo Period by a kimono store called Echigoya, which later became the Mitsukoshi department store. To get rid of extra stock, they filled bags with unused fabric and sold them at a discount during a winter sale. This became very popular, and the tradition continues today.

Another story is about Daimaruya, which later became the Daimaru department store we know. They came up with the idea of selling lucky bags during a festival and New Year's. This made the tradition spread across Japan. Also, there are some stories that claim lucky bags started in the later Meiji period. Nevertheless, no matter when it started, all stories agree that a store selling kimono fabric began this tradition.

In Japan, you can find lucky bags on shelves during the New Year. Some stores start selling them a bit earlier on December 29th. And some famous stores even ask you to reserve lucky bags months in advance!

If you miss the New Year sales, don't worry. You can always find big sales at other times during the year. When you visit Japan, keep an eye out for the Fukubukuro sign and enjoy the surprises!

Reading Comprehension: Choose the best answer for each question.

_____ 1. What is the main purpose of the passage?

    (A) To criticize the commercialization of Japanese traditions.

(B) To inform readers about the history of department stores.

(C) To describe the popularity of kimono fabric in modern Japan.

(D) To introduce and explain the tradition of Fukubukuro.

_____ 2. When do some stores in Japan start selling lucky bags?

(A) February 14th. (B) July 1st. (C) December 29th. (D) October 31st.

_____ 3. Which of the following can be inferred from the passage about the Fukubukuro tradition?

(A) It was invented by tourists who visited Japan.

(B) It was initiated by a computer accessories store.

(C) It only happens during New Year sales.

(D) It provides a fun way to get discounted items.

_____ 4. Where is this passage most likely to appear?

(A) In a travel guide about Japan.

(B) In a textbook about Japanese history.

(C) In a magazine featuring computer science.

(D) In an advertisement for department stores.

_____ 5. What is the author's attitude toward Fukubukuro?

(A) Critical. (B) Neutral. (C) Enthusiastic. (D) Indifferent.

Try it! Fill in each blank with the correct word. Make changes if necessary.

| stock | reserve | sign | purchase | discount |

1. The toy store offered a special _____ on all board games.

2. Some families will choose to _____ tickets early for the popular water park to avoid long lines.

3. The grocery store owner always makes sure there is enough fresh produce to fill the _____ .

4. If you turn left, you will see a glowing neon _____ and the entrance to the casino is right there.

5. I plan to _____ a new laptop this weekend to replace my old one.

Unit 37 Straight A's at the Cost of Sleep?

During school days, almost everyone has been through this in class: You yawned. You felt your eyelids heavy. Your upper body rocked to and fro. Your book dropped to the floor with a bang that woke up your classmates.

Studies show that a student needs at least 8 hours' sleep a day, but most students get less than that. Some parents are happy to see their kids **burn the midnight oil**. They think it is worth studying late because getting good grades is everything. So a lot of students in Taiwan wake up at 6 a.m., leave school at 6 p.m., come home from cram schools at 10 p.m., and still have more work to do at home! They barely get a good night's sleep, and this bothers some parents. These parents feel bad when they see that their kids can't focus in class, or that their kids come home tired out and stressed out.

Too much homework is what many students complain about. They say they need to spend a lot of time just catching up or getting ahead. Or many just don't know how to get their things done in a more efficient way. Many experts suggest students develop good study habits like "starting now," "concentrating in class," or forming study groups after class to help each other out. They all hope that students can sleep more while also doing well in school.

Reading Comprehension: Choose the best answer for each question.

_____ 1. The article mainly helps students _____ .
  (A) focus in class
  (B) form study groups
  (C) develop good sleeping habits
  (D) get enough sleep and do well in school at the same time

_____ 2. The first paragraph describes how a student _____ during class.

(A) dozes off   (B) gets up   (C) catches up   (D) gets ahead

_____ 3. Many students complain about _____ .

(A) getting bad grades   (B) waking up at 6 in the morning

(C) not having enough sleep   (D) having too much homework

_____ 4. The phrase "burn the midnight oil" in the second paragraph means

_____ .

(A) dozing off during class

(B) studying or working until late at night

(C) suffering as a result of doing something

(D) becoming very tired from trying to do too many things

_____ 5. Which of the following is true?

(A) Many experts suggest students develop good sleeping habits.

(B) Studies show that most students get at least 8 hours' sleep a day.

(C) Experts all hope that students can sleep more and study even harder.

(D) Some parents are happy to see their kids stay up studying, while some are not.

Try it! Fill in each blank with the correct word. Make changes if necessary.

to and fro	at least	worth	efficient	concentrate

1. The book is very interesting; it is _____ reading.
2. Feeling excited, the kids ran _____ in the hall.
3. The new washing machine is more _____ than our old one. It helps save a lot of time.
4. The ring is expensive; it costs _____ NT$10,000.
5. I couldn't _____ on my studies. My mind wandered.

Unit 38　A Dollar Saved Is a Dollar Earned

When people need more money, most of them work overtime or find a better-paid job. Yet, earning more isn't the only way to increase the money in your bank account. Instead, by spending your money wisely, you can achieve the goal without changing your job or working extra hours.

An important step in saving money is to create a budget. You should become aware of how much you earn and where you are spending your money. A practical way is carrying a small notebook around and making a note each time you buy something. Reviewing your notes, you're sure to find ways to save money. For example, coffee drinkers may find they have spent much money on buying coffee from coffee shops. Therefore, they may save money by making coffee at home instead. Using coupons is another way to cut costs. Many shoppers have found that by using coupons, they can lower their grocery bills by fifty percent.

Overall, creative thinking is what we need to save money. Besides the creative ideas mentioned above, some students have started using free Internet calling service like LINE to reduce their phone bills. By spending money wisely, you might be surprised that you have more money than you need. As the famous saying goes, "A dollar saved is a dollar earned."

Reading Comprehension: Choose the best answer for each question.

_____ 1. According to the article, the author thinks that _____ .
   (A) the best way to save money is to change jobs
   (B) using coupons is of no help in saving money
   (C) people should not go shopping at all
   (D) creative thinking is important for saving money

_____ 2. Which of the following is NOT a way to save money?

(A) Using coupons when shopping.

(B) Buying the latest model of cell phones.

(C) Shopping when things are on sale.

(D) Making coffee at home instead of buying it from coffee shops.

_____ 3. Creating a budget can help us save money because we can _____ .

(A) know how much money we make each month

(B) be more aware of how much money we are spending

(C) know where to get coupons

(D) learn how to make coffee at home

_____ 4. Which of the following is true?

(A) Having extra jobs is the only way to get more money.

(B) Creating a budget helps manage money well.

(C) To save money, some people buy clothes once a year.

(D) Changing jobs helps people reduce costs or bills.

_____ 5. Some people use LINE to reduce their _____ .

(A) grocery bills   (B) costs of coffee

(C) costs of clothing   (D) phone bills

Try it! Fill in each blank with the correct word. Make changes if necessary.

overtime	budget	instead	coupon	review

1. Dave didn't want to eat noodles. _____ , he wanted to have rice.

2. By using the _____ , I bought the pants with 20% off.

3. We have to work _____ to get the project done.

4. The watch is so expensive that it's over my _____ .

5. We'll _____ the policy to ensure the welfare of the workers.

Unit 39 Aromatherapy: Not Only for the Nose

Have you ever thought that what you smell can influence the way you feel? A new therapy called "aromatherapy" claims that smells can influence our feelings and even our health.

The word "aromatherapy" was first used by a French scientist in the 1920s. It combines the word "aroma," or smell, with "therapy," or treatment. Basically, aromatherapy uses essential oils and compounds extracted from plants. In aromatherapy, the smells of essential oils are inhaled. In other words, a person should breathe deeply while holding a bottle of essential oil close to his or her nose. Besides, essential oils can also be massaged directly into the skin or put into a hot bath.

Aromatherapy has become very popular with people who want relief from stress. What's more, a few doctors are now using aromatherapy in hospitals to relieve patients' pains, especially mothers with serious labor pains.

But some people have criticized aromatherapy. They say there is no scientific proof to show that it is really effective. In addition, some aromatherapy products smell good, but actually are fake.

Despite these criticisms, the popularity of aromatherapy continues to grow. But the debate over its usefulness continues as well. Many people wonder if aromatherapy is an effective therapy or just a way to make money. Only time will tell.

📖 **Reading Comprehension:** Choose the best answer for each question.

_____ 1. The word "aromatherapy" means _____ .

(A) a special hot bath in hospitals   (B) a way to breathe in steam

(C) traditional massage using oils   (D) treatment with essential oils

_____ 2. What kind of material is used in aromatherapy?

(A) Drugs.

(B) Compounds extracted from the sea.

(C) Water.

(D) Essential oils.

_____ 3. Which of the following is not the right way of using essential oils?

(A) To breathe them in.   (B) To massage them into one's skin.

(C) To add them to drinking water.   (D) To put them into a hot bath.

_____ 4. According to the article, who especially needs aromatherapy?

(A) A boy who keeps crying.   (B) A woman who is giving birth.

(C) A worker who hurts his fingers.   (D) A teenager who is overweight.

_____ 5. Which of the following statements is NOT true?

(A) People's feelings may be influenced by what they smell.

(B) Aromatherapy has been proved to be very effective.

(C) The debate over the usefulness of aromatherapy still continues.

(D) Some aromatherapy products that smell good may be fake.

💡**Try it!**   Fill in each blank with the correct word. Make changes if necessary.

influence	combine	breathe	criticize	relief

1. Sunlight and water are two factors _____ how plants will grow.

2. Jane's mom _____ her for her sloppy attitude toward schoolwork.

3. It's a _____ from stress to finally finish the project.

4. _____ white with black and you'll get gray.

5. Mr. Smith is a chain smoker; he sometimes has difficulty _____ .

Unit 40  All About Healthy Living

Thanks to the tendency to sit at the desk for long hours and to eat poorly, people now have thicker waistlines and develop diseases in their adulthood. Here are some tips on how to stay fit.

1. Eat healthily: A diet of whole grains, vegetables, and fruits is the best. Eating foods rich in fiber and low in "bad" fats makes you healthy. The key here is eating a proper amount of everything and sticking to this diet over a long time.

2. Stay physically active: Try to get exercise at least 30 minutes a day. For example, doing brisk walking regularly not only helps you stay in shape but reduces stress and improves sleep and memory.

However, perfect health is more a matter of balance in both the mind and the body. Here are two tips to better emotional well-being.

1. Have a support group: Stay in close contact with the important people in your life. Your family and good friends help you through life's many **ups and downs**. They can often take care of your emotional needs, and help you look at things from different angles and think more clearly.

2. Think positively: Positive thinking has been shown to produce a stronger sense of hope in people, which drives them to their goals and happier lives.

Reading Comprehension: Choose the best answer for each question.

_____ 1. The article is mainly about _____ .

    (A) how to eat healthily   (B) how to lose weight

    (C) how to stay healthy   (D) how to handle stress

_____ 2. _____ may cause disease.

    (A) A poor diet   (B) Sitting for a long time

    (C) Developing thicker waistlines   (D) All of the above.

_____ 3. Doing exercise every day may NOT help people _____ .

    (A) stay fit   (B) release stress

    (C) have a good sleep   (D) develop waistlines

_____ 4. The phrase "ups and downs" in the fifth paragraph means _____ .

    (A) one's duty or responsibility

    (B) moving upwards and downwards

    (C) a mixture of good and bad things

    (D) a change of direction

_____ 5. _____ may help people stay mentally and physically healthy.

    (A) Regular exercise

    (B) Positive thinking

    (C) Love and care from families and friends

    (D) All of the above.

Try it! Fill in each blank with the correct word. Make changes if necessary.

thanks to	stick to	stress	improve	ups and downs

1. No matter what happened, they would _____ their plan.

2. My English has greatly _____ . I also get better grades in math.

3. _____ Kent's being late, we missed the first train.

4. My friends and I have undergone many _____ in our lives together.

5. Since the final exam is coming, the students are under great _____ .

Unit 41 World Water Council: To the Rescue of Water

The World Water Council is an organization made up of members from all over the world. Its purposes are to discuss better ways to conserve, protect, and manage fresh water around the world. The members try to teach these techniques to all of the governments, large companies, and other important people that make major decisions concerning water problems around the world.

After so many successful international meetings held to solve water problems between governments, in 1995, a special committee was created to decide what the aim of the World Water Council would be. The World Water Council was then officially formed in June 1996. Its headquarters is set up in the city of Marseille, France.

Most of the World Water Council's main activities are to hold special meetings that bring important people and experts worldwide together. The World Water Council also tries to make sure that fresh water is available to everyone around the world and works hard to bring water to poor countries. **It** has formed many groups, such as the Water Cooperation Facility, and used the money from its membership to help reduce water problems around the world.

The conservation and protection of fresh water is very important to people of the world. Most governments have recognized this need and are actively helping make the projects of the World Water Council successful.

Reading Comprehension: Choose the best answer for each question.

_____ 1. This article is mainly about _____ .

    (A) the importance of water conservation

    (B) the process of making major decisions

    (C) the introduction of the World Water Council

    (D) the history of the city of Marseille

_____ 2. When was the World Water Council officially set up?

    (A) In 1977.   (B) In 1995.   (C) In 1996.   (D) In 1997.

_____ 3. The word "it" in paragraph 3 refers to _____ .

    (A) the poor country   (B) the large company

    (C) the French Government   (D) the World Water Council

_____ 4. Which of the following about the World Water Council is true?

    (A) It discusses better ways to protect water resources.

    (B) It teaches large companies how to produce drinking water.

    (C) It works hard to bring water to many developed countries.

    (D) It makes money from its membership.

_____ 5. We can know from the article that _____ .

    (A) most governments support what the World Water Council is doing

    (B) many companies do not want to help the World Water Council

    (C) people try not to be taught the techniques concerning water problems

    (D) there is no other group helping with the water problems now

Try it!   Fill in each blank with the correct word. Make changes if necessary.

purpose	manage	available	conserve	recognize

1. The doctor should _____ how serious the disease is.

2. We should _____ the environment for the people in the future.

3. The singer's new album will be _____ in stores tomorrow.

4. The _____ of this concert is to raise money for the poor.

5. The government tried to _____ the difficult situation in wartime.

Unit 42　The Gift of Giving

While I was getting things ready for the Saturday garage sale, a picture caught my eye. It was a picture of my classmates and I when we were in eight. It showed the sizes of the clothes each of us wore, and the picture touched something deep in my heart. So I had my kids, Lynn and Jessica, look at the photo and told them, "Look, so many people are so poor that they don't have the right clothes to wear. This weekend, we're going to show what a big help we can be. How about each of us gives away a few things for free?"

I told the kids to start with old stuff they didn't want anymore. Lynn took out boxes of old toy soldiers and T-shirts he grew out of. I smiled at Lynn and turned my head to see what Jessica would bring with her. There I saw her coming with her favorite doll, Gail, still new and well taken care of. "Jess, you don't have to! You love this doll so much," said I. "Mommy, if Gail can make me happy, she will make other girls happy, too. Bye now, Gail," said Jessica as she waved to her doll.

I was impressed. What Jessica just did gave me much to think about. Giving away things you don't want is easy, but sharing what you love isn't. **Putting yourselves in others' shoes** and giving them what they need most is, well, love.

Reading Comprehension: Choose the best answer for each question.

_____ 1. The article is mainly about _____ .

    (A) suitable stuff for garage sales

    (B) people who are very poor

    (C) loving and helping others unselfishly

    (D) giving away things someone doesn't want

_____ 2. What did the speaker suggest doing at the garage sale?

(A) Cleaning the garage.   (B) Making some money.

(C) Looking at pictures together.   (D) Giving away some stuff for free.

_____ 3. What did Jessica want to give away?

(A) Old T-shirts.   (B) Old toy soldiers.

(C) Her favorite doll.   (D) An old garage.

_____ 4. The phrase "put yourself in one's shoes" means _____.

(A) putting on another person's shoes

(B) doing something for one's own sake

(C) doing the job that someone used to do

(D) imagining that someone is in another person's situation

_____ 5. Which of the following is true?

(A) The doll that Jessica gave away was old and shabby.

(B) Giving away things you don't want is not easy at all.

(C) The speaker suggested that her kids give away what they loved.

(D) Jessica gave away her doll and hoped it would make other girls happy.

Try it!   Fill in each blank with the correct word. Make changes if necessary.

catch one's eye	give away	stuff	anymore	grow out of

1. The luggage is so small that George can't put all his _____ in it.

2. Richard decided to _____ all his money to the poor after death.

3. Since Judy had _____ the sweater, she gave it to her little sister.

4. I saw a woman in bright red; her dress really _____.

5. The Lins moved to Japan. They don't live in Taiwan _____.

Unit 43 Silver Economy

Our world is changing, and more and more people are growing older. This creates new opportunities for the global economy, known as the "Silver Economy." This special part of the economy focuses on producing goods and services for older people—those who are 50 years old or more.

One important part of the silver economy is tourism. Many retired people travel a lot. They visit new places, go on cruises, and stay in hotels. Some companies plan special holidays for older travelers, like trips for people over 50. What's more, some hotels and restaurants are just for older people because they understand what the elderly need.

Another essential business is healthcare. Older people often need help with medical appointments, such as going to the dentist or the hospital. Some older people live in nursing homes, where there are professionals to take care of them all day. In some countries, there are even special hospitals for older people to meet their needs.

There are also many businesses that sell products for older people. Some companies make special clothes that are easy to put on and take off. Others make special phones with big buttons and simple menus that are easier to use than normal phones. And some design cars with bigger seats and mirrors for older drivers. There are even cars that are easier to drive and park.

In the future, the silver economy will be even more important. By 2050, there will be about two billion people over 65 in the world. That's one in every four people. Therefore, businesses should begin focusing on older customers because they offer best business opportunities.

Reading Comprehension: Choose the best answer for each question.

_____ 1. What is the passage mainly about?

(A) An economy that focuses on producing precious metals.

(B) An economy that cares for women.

(C) An economy that supports all workers.

(D) An economy that produces goods for older people.

_____ 2. Which of the following describes the order of businesses mentioned in the passage?

(A) Special products → tourism → healthcare.

(B) Special products → healthcare → tourism.

(C) Tourism → healthcare → special products.

(D) Healthcare → tourism → special products.

_____ 3. Which of the following is the example of products designed for older people?

(A) Clothes that are fashionable.　　(B) Phones with high-tech features.

(C) Cars with powerful engines.　　(D) Cars with easy-to use features.

_____ 4. Which of the following is one business aspect of the silver economy?

(A) Selling toys for children.

(B) Offering travel packages for retired people.

(C) Producing high-tech products for teenagers.

(D) Creating fashion trends for young adults.

_____ 5. Which of the following is a picture of a nursing home?

(A)　　　　　　(B)　　　　　　(C)　　　　　　(D)

Try it! Fill in each blank with the correct word. Make changes if necessary.

tourism	cruise	elderly	medical	global

1. John went on a(n) _____ around the world this summer vacation.

2. _____ professionals work in hospitals to care for people's health.

3. The _____ couple took good take of themselves despite their age.

4. The outbreak of the disease had an impact on _____ economy.

5. _____ has helped the town grow and thrive.

Unit 44 A Real Renaissance Man: Leonardo da Vinci

The Italian Leonardo da Vinci was born in the Renaissance, a time in Europe from the 14th to the 17th century, which means "rebirth." It was a time of wonderful beginnings and creativity in the sciences and the arts. The learned wanted to know the world, develop their society, and do great acts. Da Vinci was a real Renaissance man: he was a wonderful math thinker, musician, painter, and inventor. Da Vinci used his great gifts to show how people were able to think and act powerfully. He was not only a man of his times but also a man of the future.

Da Vinci drew up many plans for machines and tools. Though most of his plans never became real machines, his ideas **inspired** later inventors. In fact, many of his original ideas came true hundreds of years after his death.

Da Vinci was the first to devise the machine that would become the modern-day tank; he also invented a ship that could travel underwater. Da Vinci was also interested in machines that could send people flying. It is said that his thoughts on the helicopter encouraged Igor Sikorsky, who later became a great creator of that flying machine. Da Vinci wanted humankind to reach the heavens, and he really did move people to fly.

Reading Comprehension: Choose the best answer for each question.

_____ 1. Da Vinci was NOT a _____.
  (A) math thinker   (B) musician   (C) painter   (D) politician

_____ 2. The topic of the article is about _____.
  (A) the life of Igor Sikorsky
  (B) the inventions people had during the Renaissance
  (C) the importance of Leonardo da Vinci
  (D) how Leonardo da Vinci became a great man

_____ 3. Which of the following statements about the Renaissance is NOT true?

⒜ It means "birth."

⒝ It was from the 14th to the 17th century.

⒞ It was a time of creativity in the sciences and the arts.

⒟ The learned of that time were eager to know the world.

_____ 4. The word "inspire" in the second paragraph is similar to _____ in meaning.

⒜ gather ⒝ improve ⒞ encourage ⒟ interest

_____ 5. According to the article, which of the following is true?

⒜ Da Vinci was the creator of flying machines.

⒝ Most of Da Vinci's plans became real machines.

⒞ Da Vinci used his gifts to show how people could think and act powerfully.

⒟ Igor Sikorsky was the inventor of the modern-day tank.

Try it! Fill in each blank with the correct word. Make changes if necessary.

creativity	gift	future	original	the heavens

1. It takes great _____ to produce such a special work.

2. Peter is a born actor. He has a _____ for acting.

3. After night falls, you can see lots of stars in _____ here.

4. The child proudly says he wants to be an astronaut in the _____ .

5. The _____ version of this composition lacked unity, so it was revised.

Unit 45　Keep the Pounds Off!

Each year, about 70 million Americans try to lose weight. That is almost 1 out of every 3 people in the States alone. Some people go on a diet, cutting back on desserts or greasy foods. Others go jogging or work out in fitness centers. Still others go so far as to have cosmetic surgery. Obviously, losing weight means a lot of work. It also pulls a lot of money out of one's pockets. You may wonder now why so many Americans bother to lose weight.

It's all about "staying in shape." For many, the other word for "good-looking" is "thin." Others want better health after hearing all the bad news on **obesity**.

Almost everyone wants a fast and painless way to lose weight. Shelves of how-to books have been written to help those dying to take off a few pounds.

Losing weight can be costly. Fitness centers like Club One Fitness in Oakland, California, offer both group and personal training classes. Members can pay up to hundreds of dollars every day. They typically exercise a lot and eat just a little. A woman named Lois said she had lost 5 pounds the 5th day into such a program. It took around $300 to lose each pound, but "It's worth it," she said.

Reading Comprehension: Choose the best answer for each question.

_____ 1. The article is mainly about _____ .
　　(A) going on a diet
　　(B) taking exercise
　　(C) staying in shape
　　(D) having cosmetic surgery

_____ 2. Which of the following can help lose weight?

(A) Eating just a little.

(B) Taking exercise regularly.

(C) Cutting back on desserts or greasy foods.

(D) All of the above.

_____ 3. Why do people want to lose weight?

(A) Because many people are doing so.

(B) Because they want to be good-looking.

(C) Because it pulls a lot of money out of their pockets.

(D) Because they don't want to receive any cosmetic surgery.

_____ 4. The word "obesity" in paragraph 2 means very _____ in an unhealthy way.

(A) fat   (B) thin   (C) skinny   (D) slim

_____ 5. Which of the following is true?

(A) Fitness centers offer only group training classes.

(B) It requires lots of effort and money to lose weight.

(C) There are few books telling people how to lose weight.

(D) A woman named Lois thought losing weight cost her too much.

Try it!   Fill in each blank with the correct word. Make changes if necessary.

surgery	obviously	bother	greasy	up to

1. I won't be home tonight, so you don't even _____ to call.

2. After the interview, Carl looked upset; _____, he didn't get the job.

3. The hall can seat _____ 1,000 people.

4. To remove the tumor, the doctor was doing _____ on the patient's chest.

5. You'd better stop eating _____ heavy food. It's bad for your health.

Unit 46 The Straw That Breaks the Camel's Back

There was once an Arab traveling on a camel in the desert. When the sun set, he stopped to put up his tent, made a fire and got ready to sleep.

Half asleep, he felt a kick on his tent. He turned his head and found the camel poking its head inside the tent. "My head needs to stay in the tent to keep warm, please. It's freezing outside," the camel begged. "**Be my guest**," said the kind-hearted Arab and then went back to sleep.

It wasn't long before he felt a push on his tent. It was the camel kicking again. "Master," the camel said, "my head is warm now, but my neck is still cold. Mind if I keep it inside, too?" "Not at all," answered the Arab. But this time he felt a bit crowded.

Just as he was about to fall asleep, the camel gave the tent another kick. This time, the camel asked to keep his front legs inside. The Arab moved over to make room for the camel, but it was no longer that comfortable inside the tent.

Now the camel kicked the Arab hard in the face, shouting, "The tent is too small for two. Leave this tent and get lost!" With that, the camel gave a kick, sending the poor Arab into the air.

 Reading Comprehension: Choose the best answer for each question.

_____ 1. Which of the sayings can be used to sum up the story?

(A) Seeing is believing.

(B) Haste makes waste.

(C) A bad penny always comes back.

(D) Give him an inch and he'll take a yard.

_____ 2. From the context, we can infer that the weather was _____ after sunset.

    (A) hot   (B) windy   (C) rainy   (D) chilly

_____ 3. Why did the camel kick the tent again and again?

    (A) Because it was afraid of the dark.

    (B) Because the Arab treated it badly.

    (C) Because it wanted to wake up the Arab.

    (D) Because it wanted to have the tent all to itself.

_____ 4. The phrase "be my guest" in paragraph 2 means _____.

    (A) feeling comfortable and relaxed

    (B) being unwilling to share something with someone

    (C) being the most important person invited to an event

    (D) giving someone permission to do what he or she has asked to do

_____ 5. The article is probably from _____.

    (A) a scientific journal   (B) a storybook

    (C) a computer magazine   (D) an academic report

Try it!   Fill in each blank with the correct word. Make changes if necessary.

put up	freezing	be about to	make room	get lost

1. Put your coat on; it's _____ outside.

2. My sister always wants me to _____ whenever she is studying.

3. The box is too small. How can you _____ for all these books?

4. The fence was _____ to keep the lambs inside.

5. The meeting _____ begin, but I still need some time to get ready!

Unit 47   The Challenges of Crowdfunding

Are you ready to turn your big idea into a real business? Finding the proper funding is crucial for success. Crowdfunding is a way for entrepreneurs to get money for their startups. But it's not always easy. Let's explore the challenges and how to overcome them.

One challenge is getting people interested in your company and dealing with their expectations. Some investors may only look at the future and not at how your startup has been doing so far, so they may expect too much of you. To fix this, be clear about your company and how your product works.

Another challenge is that not all investors know how crowdfunding works. They might not trust you in the beginning. You can solve this by knowing your business well and explaining why they should invest in your startup.

Also, deciding how much money to raise can be tricky. It's not just about what you need but also about your company's value. Talk to other people who've done this before to get an idea. Be careful not to ask for too much.

In addition, there are many crowdfunding platforms, but not all are the same. Some are better for new startups, while others are for companies with stable products. Try different platforms, ask questions, and don't use too many.

Lastly, keeping your idea safe is important. Investors need enough information to understand your startup, but don't give them more than they need. Protect parts of your idea with copyright laws and make people sign agreements not to reveal important information.

If you understand these challenges and get well prepared for them, you can do better at raising funds for your startup. Good luck!

Reading Comprehension: Choose the best answer for each question.

_____ 1. What is the main idea of this passage?

(A) The importance of finding the proper funding.

(B) Challenges and solutions in crowdfunding for startups.

(C) Exploring different business models.

(D) How copyright laws protect startup ideas.

_____ 2. According to the passage, what is the challenge you may face when you get people interested in your company?

(A) Investors expecting too much.　　(B) Lack of a good business model.

(C) Not knowing what people want.　　(D) Choosing the right platform.

_____ 3. Which of the following can be inferred from the advice on deciding how much money to raise for a startup?

(A) Always ask for more than needed.

(B) The value of the company is irrelevant.

(C) Your needs decide everything.

(D) Seek advice from experienced individuals.

_____ 4. How does the author begin the passage?

(A) By giving a definition.　　　　(B) By asking a question.

(C) By providing statistics.　　　　(D) By comparing people's responses.

_____ 5. Which of the following best describes the author's attitude toward the future of crowdfunding?

(A) Amazed.　　　(B) Doubtful.　　　(C) Hopeful.　　　(D) Conservative.

Try it!　Fill in each blank with the correct word. Make changes if necessary.

expectation	platform	challenge	invest	reveal

1. Starting a new game can be a real _____, but it's exciting!

2. At Sam's birthday party, there's always a big _____ for fun.

3. My mom thinks it is a good idea to _____ in stocks.

4. This old software can only be run on PC _____, so you can't use it on your phone.

5. Magicians often use a magic trick to _____ something special during their shows.

Unit 48 Wait a Minute. Do I Need to Buy This?

As you stand in line at the supermarket, you notice some chocolate bars near the checkouts. A sign says they are new, so you pick up a few. Then, you also buy some gum, which is on sale, and some toys for the children, too. When you return home, you discover that you have bought things that were not on your shopping list, and because of the impulse buying, you've spent more money than you had planned.

When people buy something on impulse, it is called impulse buying. These items are often found on display tables at the front of stores and, more commonly, near checkouts, where customers must wait in line. Some common impulse buying includes candies, chocolate, gum, toys, etc.

Impulse buying is usually made very quickly. Shop owners use special displays with phrases like "low price," "free," and "on sale" to attract shoppers who want to find good deals. Signs that say "limited time offer" or "one day only" also encourage shoppers to make a fast decision.

Surprisingly, up to 40 percent of the products people buy in stores are not in their shopping plan at all, according to one report. So, it seems clear that as long as people keep buying things on impulse, stores will make it easy for them to do so.

Reading Comprehension: Choose the best answer for each question.

_____ 1. Which of the following items is NOT commonly bought on impulse?
　　(A) Bread.　　　(B) Candies.　　　(C) Chocolate.　　　(D) Gum.

_____ 2. According to the article, what is "impulse buying"?

(A) People buy something like chocolate, candies, or toys.

(B) People buy something when they see it, but they never planned to buy it.

(C) People push themselves into buying something they don't like.

(D) People buy things at a very low price.

_____ 3. Where do shoppers often find impulse buying?

(A) At the magazine section.　　　(B) At the bread section.

(C) Near the checkouts.　　　(D) Beside a large sign.

_____ 4. Which of the following is NOT true about impulse buying?

(A) Impulse buys are usually not on one's shopping list.

(B) Store owners encourage impulse buying.

(C) Impulse buying is often made very quickly.

(D) A sign that says "one day only" cannot encourage impulse buying.

_____ 5. What might be your thought when you make impulse buying?

(A) "I have to stop buying anything. I must save money."

(B) "I must buy this. It is on sale now."

(C) "I must make a shopping list next time."

(D) "I will think twice before buying it."

Try it!　Fill in each blank with the correct word. Make changes if necessary.

notice　　customer　　limited　　offer　　decision

1. It's the goal of the restaurant to _____ the best food and service.
2. Maggie made the _____ to leave the company.
3. It's worthwhile to get a copy of the book since it's a _____ edition.
4. Bill was so insensitive that he didn't _____ his girlfriend was mad.
5. Kim is a regular _____ of that bookstore. She often goes there to buy books.

Unit 49　Juggling Life's Glass and Rubber Balls

Professor Goodwin stood in front with several items on the desk: a jar, some golf balls, stones, sand, and a mug. He first put the golf balls into the jar and asked, "Class, is this jar full?" "Yeah," we all agreed. Then he put into the jar some little stones, which filled the openings between the golf balls. "Now, is the jar full?" Mr. Goodwin threw the same question at us. "Sure," we answered. Then he poured the sand into the jar and asked again, and we said, "It's full already."

Finally, he tilted the mug and a brown liquid flowed right into the jar. We were all curious about what that meant. "Now," said Mr. Goodwin, "I'd like you to see this jar as your life. The golf balls are the things that matter the most: family, friends, health and your passion. With them, your life is still full when everything else is lost. The stones are like your job, your house and car—the less important things in your life. The sand is the small stuff, things that are unimportant."

"If you put the sand in first," he went on, "there's no room for the balls or stones. This is also true to life. If you **get stuck on** something of little importance, you have no room for great things."

I raised my hand and asked what that brown liquid was and stood for. Professor smiled, saying: "It's coffee. It means however full everyday life is, there's always room for you to have a cup of coffee with your friends."

Reading Comprehension: Choose the best answer for each question.

_____ 1. The article is mainly about how to _____.

    (A) make coffee   (B) do an experiment

    (C) make one's life full   (D) handle trivia in one's life

_____ 2. The stones refer to _____.

    (A) jobs   (B) families   (C) friends   (D) All of the above.

_____ 3. According to Professor Goodwin, what is the most important thing in one's life?

    (A) Health.   (B) Passion.   (C) Friendship.   (D) All of the above.

_____ 4. The phrase "get stuck on" in paragraph 3 means _____.

    (A) being unable to move from a place

    (B) being unable to escape from a bad situation

    (C) having something unwanted because someone cannot get rid of it

    (D) being unable to do any more of something that someone is working on

_____ 5. Which of the following is true?

    (A) The jar refers to one's life.

    (B) The sand refers to something of great importance in one's life.

    (C) The golf balls refer to something of little importance in one's life.

    (D) One's job, house and car is the most important things in life.

Try it! Fill in each blank with the correct word. Make changes if necessary.

pour	liquid	curious	passion	stand for

1. The kid is _____ about everything, so he keeps asking questions.
2. Vincent has a _____ for baseball. He not only watches baseball games but also plays baseball.
3. The table was covered with some _____ which looked like water.
4. The word WHO _____ the World Health Organization.
5. The waiter _____ some coffee into my cup.

American vs. British English

Americans and Britons both speak English for sure. But there are actually some differences between American and British English.

First, they sound quite differently. Americans like to link words as they speak. For example, you may hear an American say "I gotta go" instead of "I got to go," and "Gotcha!" rather than "Got you!" British people, on the contrary, speak more clearly and distinctly.

In American and British English, the same word may have different meanings. On the other hand, different words may mean the same thing. At the end of a meal with an American friend, you say "May I have the check, please" but you would call a British waiter and say, "Can I have the bill, please?" Or, an American may tell you "I want to take a vacation" while a Briton would use "holiday" instead.

All these differences might be overwhelming for a student of English, but English is not alone. People speaking the same language develop their own habits of using that language when they do not live close to one another. Besides, languages are like living beings. They grow and change. On different lands, the same language can change in a different way, and English is a perfect example.

Reading Comprehension: Choose the best answer for each question.

_____ 1. The article is mainly about _____.

    (A) the development of English in the U.S.

    (B) the cultural differences between the U.S. and the U.K.

    (C) the reasons why Americans and Britons both speak English

    (D) the differences between American English and British English

_____ 2. Which of the following is used by Americans?

(A) "I gotta go."   (B) "Gotcha!"   (C) "Check."   (D) All of the above.

_____ 3. Which of the following is true?

(A) Britons tend to pause between words as they speak.

(B) In American English and British English, different words may have the same meaning.

(C) The phrase "take a holiday" is commonly used by Americans.

(D) There is no grammatical difference between American English and British English.

_____ 4. Which of the following is used by Britons?

(A) "Stand in line."   (B) "I gotta go."

(C) "Can I have the bill, please?"   (D) "I just had a vacation."

_____ 5. Which of the following is NOT true?

(A) In different places, the same language may change differently.

(B) Languages never grow and change.

(C) Americans and Britons sometimes use different expressions to refer to the same thing.

(D) In American English and British English, the same word may have different meanings.

Try it! Fill in each blank with the correct word. Make changes if necessary.

| quite | besides | for sure | difference | on the contrary |

1. None of us knew _____ when Tony would arrive.

2. The hotel room was _____ dirty and I couldn't stand it anymore.

3. The hospital thought the disease was under control; _____ , more people died because of it.

4. I like the movie. The story is interesting; _____ , the music is great.

5. What's the _____ between a moth and a butterfly?

 Note

ANSWER KEY

1 DAAAB 1. balance 2. turn out 3. generations 4. in fact 5. think of

2 DBCCB 1. talent 2. harmful 3. concerned 4. attention 5. entertainment

3 DDDCC 1. When it comes to 2. cut off 3. decorated 4. make it 5. various

4 BCADB 1. remote 2. Digital 3. arrange 4. explore 5. flexible

5 CDBCD 1. property 2. admitted 3. estimated 4. crimes 5. in particular

6 BDADB 1. attention 2. affair 3. audience 4. morals 5. tradition

7 DDAAB 1. characteristic 2. embraced 3. convince 4. encourage 5. exchange

8 CAADD 1. distance 2. detect 3. developed 4. a great deal 5. is likely to

9 BDABD 1. appropriate 2. appeared 3. at ease 4. tension 5. moderate

10 DDABA 1. affect 2. absorb 3. expressed 4. reduce 5. pollution

11 DDCAB 1. celebrities 2. struggle 3. breakdown 4. shared 5. support

12 ADBDA 1. To begin with 2. take on 3. look down on 4. a couple of
            5. in common

13 DDDDB 1. confidence 2. approached 3. surroundings 4. became used to
            5. attractive

14 ACDBB 1. interactive 2. touchless 3. decrease 4. tasks 5. convenience

15 BBBCD 1. leads to 2. familiar 3. downtown 4. at last 5. allowed

16 DDCDC 1. message 2. in a good mood 3. put out 4. pull over 5. communicate

17 CBADC 1. outgoing 2. suitable 3. predict 4. measure 5. reliable

18 DCBAB 1. Check out 2. terror 3. Once upon a time 4. enthusiasm 5. located

19 CCDAB 1. imagination 2. creative 3. come out 4. friendship 5. captured

20 ABBBA 1. scared 2. conquer 3. then and there 4. grabbed 5. ate up

21 AABCC 1. discover 2. consuming 3. made a fortune 4. production 5. traced back

22 ADDDB 1. competition 2. speak up 3. feature 4. direct 5. hint

23 ACDDC 1. complete 2. journey 3. opted for 4. used to 5. advantages

24 DBCCA 1. According to 2. wheat 3. buried 4. claimed 5. debate

25 CDBCC 1. comforts 2. tent 3. switch off 4. give up 5. option

26 DDBDB 1. emergency 2. is full of 3. imagine 4. as soon as 5. location

27 BBBDB 1. battle 2. Alarmed 3. broke out 4. attack 5. silence

28 CDBAA 1. walks of life 2. crash 3. project 4. unity 5. interviewed

29 BDCCB 1. image 2. famous 3. lightning 4. device 5. inventor

30 ADDBD 1. chilly 2. soul 3. tune 4. feathers 5. ask...of

31 ADBAC 1. nonsense 2. came into play 3. translating 4. look up 5. working on

32 BCDDA 1. forecast 2. struck 3. organization 4. warning 5. catch up with

33 CABDA 1. crisis 2. survived 3. die out 4. end up 5. shrank

34 BDBCA 1. adopt 2. shelter 3. volunteered 4. cuddle 5. happiness

35 BDDAB 1. fell over 2. actually 3. reached for 4. of my own 5. unbelievable

36 DCDAC 1. discount 2. reserve 3. stock 4. sign 5. purchase

37 DADBD 1. worth 2. to and fro 3. efficient 4. at least 5. concentrate

38 DBBBD 1. Instead 2. coupon 3. overtime 4. budget 5. review

39 DDCBB 1. influencing 2. criticized 3. relief 4. Combine 5. breathing

40 CDDCD 1. stick to 2. improved 3. Thanks to 4. ups and downs 5. stress

41 CCDAA 1. recognize 2. conserve 3. available 4. purpose 5. manage

42 CDCDD 1. stuff 2. give away 3. grown out of 4. caught my eye 5. anymore

43 DCDBB 1. cruise 2. Medical 3. elderly 4. global 5. Tourism

44 DCACC 1. creativity 2. gift 3. the heavens 4. future 5. original

45 CDBAB 1. bother 2. obviously 3. up to 4. surgery 5. greasy

46 DDDDB 1. freezing 2. get lost 3. make room 4. put up 5. is about to

47 BADBC 1. challenge 2. expectation 3. invest 4. platforms 5. reveal

48 ABCDB 1. offer 2. decision 3. limited 4. notice 5. customer

49 CADDA 1. curious 2. passion 3. liquid 4. stands for 5. poured

50 DDBCB 1. for sure 2. quite 3. on the contrary 4. besides 5. differences

英文成語典故Tell Me Why

李佳琪　編著

學習英文成語就像 a piece of cake！

・統整超過400個常見且實用，以典故、由來的方式，介紹背後蘊含的歷史背景與文化。
・成語按照A～Z排列，更在書末附上索引，方便尋找特定成語。
・每三回附贈一回「單元測驗」，閱讀過後可以即時檢驗。

國家圖書館出版品預行編目資料

Basic Reading: 悅讀養成／三民英語編輯小組彙編.－
－二版一刷.－－臺北市：三民，2024
面；　公分.－－（Reading Power系列）

ISBN 978-957-14-7737-4 （平裝）
1. 英語 2. 讀本

805.18　　　　　　　　　　　　112021110

 Reading Power 系列

Basic Reading：悅讀養成

彙　　　編	三民英語編輯小組
發 行 人	劉振強
出 版 者	三民書局股份有限公司
地　　　址	臺北市復興北路 386 號 (復北門市)
	臺北市重慶南路一段 61 號 (重南門市)
電　　　話	(02)25006600
網　　　址	三民網路書店 https://www.sanmin.com.tw
出版日期	初版一刷 2009 年 7 月
	二版一刷 2024 年 1 月
書籍編號	S808220
I S B N	978-957-14-7737-4

三民書局

★ 108課綱、全民英檢初／中級適用

Basic Reading:
悅讀養成 二版

三民英語編輯小組　彙編

解析夾冊

三民書局

1 生命之鍊
A Chain of Life

很久以前，在一個小村莊裡，有件事情讓農夫們憂慮不已：老鷹正不斷吃掉農場上的雞隻。除了殺死老鷹之外，他們想不出其他拯救雞隻的方法。所以，他們圍捕所有的老鷹並殺死它們。

但不久之後，他們就面臨另一個問題：數量過多的田鼠充斥在農場上，結果把農作物都吃掉了！農夫們並不知道，老鷹不只吃雞，也吃田鼠，事實上，吃掉田鼠的數量比雞還多。所以，殺死老鷹的結果是擾亂了大自然的平衡。

人們初次移居到某個地方時也會發生這種情況。人們往往為了開闢空間而砍伐野生草木，卻不知道許多動物得靠這些植物存活。若動物們沒有足夠植物作為食物，就會死亡或被迫遷徙，而大自然的平衡很容易就會被破壞。為了下一代著想，我們必須盡一切努力維護大自然的平衡、保護我們的地球。

1. 本篇文章主旨為何？
   (A) 老鷹是危險動物。
   (B) 野生動物沒有足夠植物可作為食物。
   (C) 殺死老鷹會破壞大自然的平衡。
   (D) 我們應該盡一切努力維護大自然的平衡。
   → 選項 A 不相關，選項 B、C 太狹隘。

2. 農夫們為何要殺死老鷹？
   (A) 因為老鷹吃掉他們的雞隻。
   (B) 因為老鷹吃掉他們的農作物。
   (C) 因為田鼠太多了。
   (D) 因為老鷹太多了。

3. 農夫們殺光老鷹後，結果如何？
   (A) 田鼠在他們的田地裡出沒。
   (B) 有太多雞了。
   (C) 其他野生動物死亡或被迫遷徙了。
   (D) 其他野生動物沒有足夠食物可吃。
   → overrun 表示「(蟲害等) 侵擾」，相當於 infest。

4. 在第二段中的「upset」意指 _____。
   (A) 使一項計畫或狀況出錯
   (B) 使某人感到不快樂或心煩
   (C) 使某人跌下床
   (D) 使某人身體不適
   → upset 可以表示「使心煩意亂」、「打翻」、「使 (腸胃) 不適」，於此表示「打亂，攪亂」。

5. 下列敘述何者正確？
   (A) 老鷹吃下的雞比田鼠多。
   (B) 大自然的平衡很容易遭到破壞。
   (C) 殺死老鷹有助維護大自然的平衡。
   (D) 農夫殺死所有的老鷹是為了要拯救田鼠和農作物。

> **Try it!**
> 1. balance   2. turn out   3. generations
> 4. in fact   5. think of

balance　n.　平衡	village　n.　村子	disturb　v.　擾亂
turn out　結果	eagle　n.　老鷹	field　n.　田地
generation　n.　世代	round up　圍捕	protect　v.　保護
in fact　事實上	overrun　v.　侵擾	wild　adj.　野生的
think of　想到	upset　v.　打亂	to come　將來的

2 短影音趨勢
Short-form Video Trends

在當今快步調的世界中，短影音成為我們數位娛樂的明星。它們通常持續不到一分鐘！由於智慧型手機以及抖音和 IG 等應用程式，這些短影音已經吸引了數百萬次觀看。幾乎任何擁有智慧型手機的人都可以輕鬆創作和分享這些影片。

這些短影音從娛樂到教育有多種用途。創作者可以製作短影音讓讓觀眾開懷大笑或者展現自己的跳舞或歌唱才華。而且，有些人甚至提供有關烹飪、自己動手做計畫的快速指導或分享動態消息。這些短影音的一大優點是它們像病毒一樣快速地傳播。這意味著當人們分享它們時，它們在網路上傳播得非常快。這可以吸引數百萬人觀看。對於製作影片的人來說，這可能意味著出名，甚至可以透過廣告賺錢。

然而，有些人擔心這些短影音可能會讓我們的注意力持續時間變更短或思考得不夠多。其他人則擔心惡意或有害內容的傳播。因此，謹慎並以積極的方式使用這些影片非常重要。

總之，短影音改變了我們在線上製作、觀看和分享影片的方式。它們非常受歡迎，而且看起來它們將繼續成為我們網路活動的重要一環。

1. 這篇文章主要講了什麼內容？
   (A) 抖音和 IG 的比較。
   (B) 短影音對孩子的負面影響。
   (C) 創作者製作短影音面臨的挑戰。
   (D) 數位時代短影音的流行。

2. 第二段的「go viral」是什麼意思？
   (A) 看清楚。
   (B) 傳播迅速。
   (C) 輕鬆查看。
   (D) 定期發文。

3. 這篇文章的目的為何？
   (A) 突顯短片創作者的成功。
   (B) 批評短影音的負面影響。
   (C) 指出短影音的隱憂與優點。
   (D) 展示人們如何使用短影音來宣傳產品。

4. 下列哪一項最能描述作者對短影音未來的態度？
   (A) 生氣。
   (B) 值得懷疑。
   (C) 充滿希望。
   (D) 保守。

5. 根據本文，人們對短影音有哪些擔憂？
   (A) 它們可能使我們花更多時間在網路上。
   (B) 他們可能會宣揚負面內容。
   (C) 它們可能會影響畫面品質。
   (D) 他們可能會限制我們對行動裝置的使用。

Try it!

1. talent　　2. harmful　　3. concerned
4. attention　　5. entertainment

---

talent n. 才能	harmful adj. 有害的	attract v. 吸引
entertainment n. 娛樂	concerned adj. 擔心的	show off 展示；炫耀
attention n. 注意	digital adj. 數位的	spread v. 散佈

3 在日本「放風箏」
"Go Fly a Kite" in Japan

在日本，放風箏的傳統已經超過一千年之久。日本的風箏以各種動物為形狀，從蝙蝠到蜜蜂或鳥都有，大多數風箏上都有圖畫裝飾。

說到風箏，日本有很多與風箏相關的有趣故事。有一個故事是關於一名小偷想用一個巨大的風箏來偷金子，因為金子被藏在一座高塔頂上。在一個風大的晚上，他乘著風箏抵達塔頂，在同夥的協助下，一起把金子偷走了。另一個故事是關於一對父子，他們在日本附近一座小島上遇難了，最後那名兒子靠著父親親手做出的風箏回到日本。

除此之外，年輕人之間還會舉行風箏比賽，看誰能把對手的風箏線切斷，直到最後只有一個風箏留在天空中為止。

1. 本篇文章主要是關於 _____。
 (A) 風箏比賽
 (B) 不同形狀的風箏
 (C) 與偷金子有關的日本故事
 (D) 日本的放風箏傳統
 → 選項 A、B、C 都太狹隘。

2. 在日本，風箏常做成 _____ 的形狀。
 (A) 蝙蝠 　　　　 (B) 蜜蜂
 (C) 鳥 　　　　 **(D) 以上皆是。**

3. 在上述日本故事裡，為何小偷要用風箏偷金子？
 (A) 因為他喜愛風箏比賽。
 (B) 因為風箏有各種形狀。
 (C) 因為他非常喜歡乘坐風箏。
 (D) 因為金子被藏在一座高塔頂上。

4. 在風箏比賽中，參賽者必須 _____。
 (A) 乘坐風箏
 (B) 說有趣的故事
 (C) 切斷對手的風箏線
 (D) 以圖畫來裝飾自己的風箏

5. 下列敘述何者正確？
 (A) 在日本，老年人之間很流行風箏比賽。
 (B) 當所有風箏都飛上天空時，風箏比賽即結束。
 (C) 在日本故事裡，人們會乘風箏偷東西或逃走。
 (D) 日本的放風箏傳統不到一千年。

Try it!
1. When it comes to 　　 2. cut off
3. decorated 　 4. make it 　 5. various

when it comes to　當說到…	tradition　n.　傳統	top　n.　頂端
cut off　切斷	shape　n.　形狀	tower　n.　塔樓
decorate　v.　裝飾	thief　n.　竊賊	handmade　adj.　手工製的
make it　成功	steal　v.　偷竊	match　n.　競賽
various　adj.　各式各樣的	huge　adj.　巨大的	string　n.　細繩

4 數位遊牧的崛起
The Rise of Digital Nomads

數位遊牧是指可以在任何地方工作的人。他們使用智慧型手機和筆記型電腦等行動裝置與團隊溝通和工作。他們甚至可以選擇工作的時間、地點和方式。與一般上班族不同,數位遊牧過著獨立的生活方式。

由於新科技,數位遊牧不必在傳統辦公室工作。他們自己安排日程,並可以選擇最棒的工作地點。有些人喜歡早上工作,然後再休息一段時間,而有些人則喜歡在深夜工作。這一切都取決於他們。

然而,也存在一些挑戰。例如,在偏遠地區找到訊號良好的無線網路可能不容易!此外,當數位遊牧與不同國家的人一起工作時,處理時差可能會很棘手。最重要的是,他們在尋求真正的工作與生活平衡方面經常面臨挑戰,因為他們的工作和個人生活界線並不清楚。事實上,數位遊牧喜歡去峇里島、清邁和柏林等地。這些地方很不錯的原因是它們生活成本低且網路連線可靠。

隨著科技進步,更多的人可能會選擇數位遊牧生活方式。這就像擁有一份可以讓你自由並探索新地方的工作。未來的工作正在發生變化,許多人興奮地嘗試這種彈性的生活方式。

1. 這篇文章主要講了什麼內容?
　(A) 數位遊牧的未來。
　(B) <u>數位遊牧的生活方式。</u>
　(C) 成功的數位遊牧。
　(D) 數位遊牧的歷史。

2. 下列有關數位遊牧的敘述哪一項是正確的?
　(A) 他們更喜歡在一般辦公室工作。
　(B) 他們喜歡在不工作的情況下探索新的地方。
　(C) <u>他們使用行動裝置遠端工作。</u>
　(D) 他們避免使用智慧型手機和筆記型電腦。

3. 這篇文章最有可能出現在哪裡?
　(A) <u>在一本著重於遠距工作趨勢的商業雜誌中。</u>
　(B) 在一本給辦公室經理的手冊中。
　(C) 在一則以獨自旅行熱門國家為特色的廣告中。
　(D) 在一家軟體公司的網站上。

4. 數位遊牧如何安排他們的工作行程?
　(A) 他們只在早上工作。
　(B) 他們只在深夜工作。
　(C) 他們在正常上班時間工作。
　(D) <u>他們想工作就工作。</u>

5. 為什麼數位遊牧會選擇峇里島和柏林等地工作?
　(A) 因為它們的天氣很好。
　(B) <u>因為它們有良好的無線網路。</u>
　(C) 因為它們有現代化的辦公空間。
　(D) 因為它們有美麗的自然景觀。

> **Try it!**
> 1. remote　2. Digital　3. arrange
> 4. explore　5. flexible

digital　adj.　數位的	explore　v.　探索	mobile　adj.　行動的
arrange　v.　安排	flexible　adj.　彈性的	tricky　adj.　棘手的
remote　adj.　遙遠的	nomad　n.　遊牧者	reliable　adj.　可靠的

5 解開不鎖門的奧秘
Unlocking the Mystery of Doors Unlocked

　　據估計，英國有兩百萬人出門時不鎖上家門。這種健忘舉動不只限於鄉間居民，城市居民也同樣大意，幾乎十個倫敦人之中就有一個承認自己不會鎖上家門，尤其是後門。為何人們會不鎖家門，有以下幾個原因。

　　根據一項由哈里法克斯家庭保險所做的調查，有百分之十八的人相信鄰居們會幫他們看家，所以離開家時不鎖門。另外百分之十八的人表示，他們住在一個犯罪率極低的地區，所以覺得很安全。而百分之六十的人則承認自己只是健忘。約一千七百萬人也認為，當自己在家時不鎖門也沒關係，即便事實顯示，幾乎百分之五十五入侵民宅的竊案是發生在家中有人的情況之下。

1. 這篇文章主要在討論＿＿＿＿＿＿。
　(A) 為何許多英國人很健忘
　(B) 有多少入侵民宅的竊案是有人在家時發生的
　(C) 為何許多英國人不鎖家門
　(D) 城市居民如何跟鄉間居民一樣大意

2. 百分之＿＿＿＿＿＿的人承認他們只是出門時忘了把門鎖上。
　(A) 17　　(B) 18　　(C) 55　　**(D) 60**

3. 百分之＿＿＿＿＿＿的人是因為自己住在低犯罪率的區域而不鎖家門。
　(A) 17　　**(B) 18**　　(C) 55　　(D) 60

4. ＿＿＿＿＿＿百萬人自己在家裡時不會鎖門。
　(A) 2　　(B) 10　　**(C) 17**　　(D) 18

5. 下列何者是人們不鎖家門的理由？
　(A) 他們不在家。
　(B) 他們很少使用後門。
　(C) 他們住在犯罪率高的地區。
　(D) 他們的鄰居會幫他們看著房子。

Try it!
1. property　　2. admitted　　3. estimated
4. crimes　　5. in particular

---

property　n.　財產	million　n.　百萬	common　adj.　普遍的
admit　v.　承認	unlocked　adj.　沒有鎖的	simply　adv.　僅僅
estimate　v.　估計	forgetfulness　n.　健忘	insurance　n.　保險
crime　n.　罪行	neighbor　n.　鄰居	despite　prep.　儘管
in particular　特別地	keep an eye on　照料	burglary　n.　入屋盜竊

韓國連續劇橫掃中國
Korean Soaps Sweep China

韓國電視連續劇如今在中國有許多劇迷。這些戲劇被安排在黃金時段播出，許多人會匆忙趕回家，只為了能準時收看。那些趕不上的人怎麼辦？不必擔心，還有重播可以看！關於三角戀情、日常家庭事件、皇帝與皇后，還有醫生的故事都非常受歡迎。劇迷們表示，他們喜愛劇中英俊漂亮的偶像、最新時尚潮流等等。

韓國電視連續劇也廣受出生於 1940 及 1950 年代的人歡迎，不過原因不同。戲劇中展現的敬老尊賢和尊重傳統等道德觀，才是吸引他們之處。

不過，觀眾們也有所抱怨。有些人表示，他們很討厭這些節目拖戲，其他人則對滿腦子只有愛情的情侶或沒完沒了的家族爭鬥感到厭煩不已。然而，大多數人都同意，有更多戲劇選擇的同時，也讓他們在晚餐桌上有更多話題可聊。

1. 本篇文章主要在談論 _____ 。
   (A) 最新時尚潮流　　(B) **韓國電視連續劇**
   (C) 尊重傳統　　　　(D) 黃金時段電視節目

2. 許多韓國電視連續劇是關於 _____ 。
   (A) 三角戀情故事　　(B) 日常家庭事件
   (C) 皇帝和皇后　　　(D) **以上皆是。**

3. 韓國電視連續劇吸引出生在 1940 及 1950 年代的人原因在於 _____ 。
   (A) **道德觀**
   (B) 相貌姣好的演員
   (C) 演員們時尚的穿著
   (D) 無止境的家族爭鬥主題

4. 觀眾們對韓國電視連續劇的不滿是什麼？
   (A) 戲拖得太長。
   (B) 主題總是關於滿腦子只有愛情的情侶。
   (C) 主題總是關於無止境的家族爭鬥。
   (D) **以上皆是。**

5. 下列敘述何者正確？
   (A) 韓國電視連續劇只受青少年歡迎。
   (B) **若有人無法在黃金時段收看韓國電視連續劇，還可以看重播。**
   (C) 「prime time」意指最少人收看電視的時段。
   (D) 有些觀眾對韓國電視連續劇感到厭煩，因為劇情主題總是不離皇帝和皇后。
   → prime time 表示「黃金時間」，是最多觀眾觀看的時段；rerun 表示「重播」。

Try it!

1. idol　　　2. affair　　　3. audience
4. morals　　5. tradition

idol　n.　偶像	series　n.　電視影集；系列	popularity　n.　流行
affair　n.　事務	air　v.　播送	complaint　n.　抱怨
audience　n.　觀眾	prime time　黃金時段	drag　v.　拖拉
morals　n.　道德觀	rerun　n.　重播	lovesick　adj.　害相思病的
tradition　n.　傳統	love triangle　三角戀情	endless　adj.　無盡的

7 聯合世界書院
The United World School

　　聯合世界書院的學生來自世界各地。在這所學校裡，學生們一起讀書和度過閒暇時間。校方相信，這麼做能讓他們成長為有智慧、充滿關懷和友善的人。

　　在一年一度的特殊「聯合國」展演會中，學生們被鼓勵把自己文化中有代表性的東西帶來展出。在展演開始之前，學生之間會進行文化交流。校方相信，這些舉動有助於架起不同文化之間的橋樑。

　　這所學校裡的學生在某些方面可以做出自己的決定。高年級學生可以依自己的喜好穿著來上課，而低年級學生則穿自己選出的制服。然而，還是有兩個前提必須遵守：不可配戴昂貴飾品，不穿會冒犯到他人的服飾。

　　讓所有人都滿意是不可能的。但除非學生們能擁抱自身之外的文化，否則沒有其他方法能讓這個世界變得美好。

1. 本篇文章主旨為何？
　(A) 沒有方法讓所有人都滿意。
　(B) 聯合世界書院是所好學校。
　(C) 絕對不要穿戴會冒犯他人的服裝或飾品。
　(D) 擁抱其他文化，我們能讓世界變得美好。
2. 聯合世界書院希望能協助學生們 _____ 。
　(A) 擁抱自身之外的文化
　(B) 成長為有智慧、充滿關懷和友善的人
　(C) 展示自身文化中具有代表性的東西
　(D) 以上皆是。

3. _____ 有助於減少文化之間的差異。
　(A)「聯合國」秀以其之前的文化交流
　(B) 對高年級學生採行寬鬆的服裝標準
　(C) 對低年級學生採行保守的服裝標準
　(D) 以上皆是。
4. 第三段中的「respect」意指 _____ 。
　(A) 事物的某個面向
　(B) 對某人的禮貌之舉
　(C) 對某人的仰慕之情
　(D) 對某事有非常好的看法
　→ aspect 可以表示「尊敬」、「尊重」等意，本文中表示「方面」。
5. 下列敘述何者正確？
　(A)「聯合國」秀每兩年展演一次。
　(B) 聯合世界書院的學生來自不同文化背景。
　(C) 聯合世界書院的學生很少一起度過閒暇時間。
　(D) 聯合世界書院的高年級學生被允許穿戴昂貴飾品來學校。

Try it!
1. characteristic　　2. embraced
3. convinced　　　　4. encourage
5. exchange

characteristic adj. 特有的	annually adv. 每年地	precondition n. 先決條件
embrace v. 擁抱	culture n. 文化	accessory n. 配件
convinced adj. 深信	gap n. 差異	offense n. 冒犯
encourage v. 鼓勵	bridge v. 縮減距離	outfit n. 全套服裝
exchange n. 交流；交換	uniform n. 制服	unless conj. 除非

8 音速 vs. 光速
Sound Speed vs. Light Speed

你上一次把石頭扔進水裡是什麼時候？你知道波紋是如何產生的嗎？當石頭接觸水面時，波紋即產生，而後開始向外擴散。

聲音在空氣中移動需要時間，就像水中的波紋一樣，聲音以震波的形式在分子間移動，而且它需要介質，如空氣，才能移動。有時我們尚未看見或聽見即將到來的火車，但如果我們將耳朵貼近鐵軌，就可以聽見火車正在移動的聲音。這告訴我們，聲音透過如木材、金屬等固體移動的速度比在空氣中快。

然而，光並不需要任何介質來移動。你可能已經發現，在雷聲驟然大響之前，閃電會先出現，這是因為光移動的速度比聲音快很多。光每秒能移動超過 300,000,000 公尺，而聲音則只移動約 340 公尺。這也是為何你會先看到事情的發生，之後才聽到發生當時的聲音。

1. 本篇文章主要是關於 ＿＿＿＿＿＿。
   (A) 光如何移動
   (B) 波紋如何形成
   (C) 為何聲音移動的速度比光慢
   (D) 為何把石頭扔進水裡能產生波紋

2. 就如同震波在分子間移動、波紋在水中擴散，聲音 ＿＿＿＿＿＿。
   (A) 需要時間來移動
   (B) 會移動很長的距離
   (C) 每秒移動 340 公尺
   (D) 在雷聲驟然大響之前出現

3. 第三段的「crack」意指 ＿＿＿＿＿＿。
   (A) 一聲巨響
   (B) 一個狹窄的空間或開口
   (C) 一記發出聲響的重擊
   (D) 當某物件破裂時，表面出現的細紋
   → crack 可以表示「縫隙」、「重擊」、「裂痕」，本文意思是「巨響」。

4. 光以 ＿＿＿＿＿＿ 的速度移動。
   (A) 每秒 340 公尺
   (B) 每分鐘 340 公尺
   (C) 每分鐘 300,000,000 公尺
   (D) 每秒 300,000,000 公尺

5. 下列敘述何者正確？
   (A) 雷聲會在閃電出現之前傳出。
   (B) 我們會先聽見事件發生的聲音，之後才看到事件的發生。
   (C) 聲音移動的速度比光快得多。
   (D) 以上皆非。

> **Try it!**
> 1. distance　　2. detect　　3. developed
> 4. a great deal　5. is likely to

distance n. 距離	throw v. 丟	molecule n. 分子
detect v. 察覺	wave n. 波紋	medium n. 介質；媒介
develop v. 發展	form v. 形成	solid n. 固體
a great deal 大量的	spread v. 擴展	metal n. 金屬
be likely to 可能	vibration n. 震動	crack n. 爆裂聲

9 身體會說話
Body Talk

當我們看到其他人的肢體語言時，會對他們有不同看法。同樣地，我們的肢體語言也可以表達自己。臉、手和眼睛，比起說出口的話更能說明我們內心的想法。

臉部對於顯現我們內在想法非常重要，臉能表現出我們心中沒興趣或有壓力的感受。通常，一抹微笑能表現出對他人的好意，並使他人認為我們溫暖而友善。

眼睛也能表現出我們心裡的感覺。一個強烈的眼神可能意味著有興趣、憤怒或恐懼。不直接看對方的眼睛可能意味著某人生性害羞。穩定的眼神接觸則表示一個人感到舒適自在。

將手張開的動作使人顯得誠實，適當的手勢能強調說話的內容。穩健的手勢能使人看來抱持著興趣，而過多的手勢則顯示出緊張和壓力。

我們的肢體動作表達出內心想法，並能讓別人知道我們心裡在想什麼。因此，使用適當的身體語言很重要。

1. 根據文章內容，我們的臉部 _____ 。
   (A) 絲毫不顯示我們的真正感受
   (B) 能告訴他人我們的內心想法
   (C) 只顯現出壓力和沒興趣
   (D) 使人們認為我們溫暖而友善
2. 若你跟人們說話不看他們的眼睛，他們可能會認為 _____ 。
   (A) 你不喜歡他們
   (B) 你在生氣
   (C) 你並不想跟他們說話
   (D) 你生性害羞
3. 第四段中「tension」的字意近似 _____ 。
   (A) 緊張　(B) 沒興趣　(C) 動作　(D) 重要性
4. 下列關於手勢的敘述，何者正確？
   (A) 若人們說話時雙手並未張開，表示他們不誠實。
   (B) 一個人若說話時手勢很多，可能是個容易擔心的人。
   (C) 只有右手的動作能強調一個人所說的話。
   (D) 若一個人在說謊，該人的手會動得很快。
5. 本篇文章的主旨為何？
   (A) 若我們使用肢體語言，就根本不需要說話了。
   (B) 我們使用愈多身體語言，愈能夠瞭解彼此。
   (C) 我們需要練習微笑，因為它是最好的語言。
   (D) 若能在適當時機運用肢體語言，我們就能讓別人知道自己的感受。

Try it!
1. appropriate　2. appeared　3. at ease
4. tension　5. moderate

appropriate　adj.　適合的	inner　adj.　內在的	movement　n.　動作
appear　v.　顯得	disinterest　n.　沒興趣	honest　adj.　誠實的
at ease　鬆了一口氣的	directly　adv.　直接地	add　v.　加上
tension　n.　緊張	regular　adj.　經常的	stress　n.　壓力
moderate　adj.　中庸的	eye contact　眼神接觸	therefore　adv.　因此

10 空氣汙染四處瀰漫
Air Pollution Is "in the Air"

長久以來，科學家們一直憂心空氣汙染對自然界的影響，近來甚至還有室內空氣不一定比室外空氣乾淨的擔憂出現。待在建築物中過久的人們可能會頭昏、易打瞌睡，並且容易感冒。這種症狀就叫做「病態建築症候群」。

科學家們指出，今日的房屋本身就是某些汙染的來源，這項事實直到 1970 年代早期才被注意到。建商因為想減少預算而選擇人造材料當建材，結果使住戶們暴露在吸入這些建材所散發出的有害氣體的危險下。

人們在空氣汙染持續惡化的同時，不斷尋求解決之道。有些科學家後來發現，答案其實就在大自然裡：綠色植物。

科學家們認為，植物的葉子能在釋出氧氣的同時減少汙染源。對植物所進行的許多研究發現，不同的植物會吸收不同化學物質。因此，植物種類越多，空氣品質也會越好。

1. 本篇文章主要是關於 _____ 。
   (A) 各種汙染
   (B) 影響大自然的空氣汙染
   (C) 人造建材的使用
   (D) 建材所釋出的汙染源
   → 選項 A 太廣泛，選項 B、C 與內文關係不大。

2. 為何房屋會是汙染的來源？
   (A) 因為能源的使用。
   (B) 因為植物生長於室內。
   (C) 因為室外有空氣汙染。
   (D) 因為人造建材的使用。

3. 有些建商使用人造建材因為他們
   _____ 。
   (A) 想減少成本
   (B) 擔心空氣汙染會影響大自然
   (C) 發現植物會吸收不同化學物質
   (D) 害怕住戶可能吸入有害氣體

4. 室內汙染問題的解決之道會是什麼？
   (A) 化學物質。　　**(B) 綠色植物。**
   (C) 新型態的能源。　(D) 新型態的建材。

5. 下列敘述何者正確？
   (A) 有些植物會吸收化學物質。
   (B) 有些植物會釋放有害氣體。
   (C) 只有少數種類的植物能使室內空氣品質變好。
   (D) 1970 年代之前，人們就已經意識到房屋是某些汙染的來源。

> **Try it!**
> 1. affect   2. absorb   3. expressed
> 4. reduce   5. pollution

affect v. 影響	concern n. 擔心	material n. 材料
absorb v. 吸收	dizzy adj. 頭昏的	dweller n. 居住者
express v. 表達	syndrome n. 症候群	inhale v. 吸入
reduce v. 減少	budget n. 預算	solution n. 解決之道
pollution n. 汙染	artificial adj. 人工的	chemical n. 化學製品

名人與社交焦慮症
Celebrities and Social Anxiety

過著有社交焦慮的生活會讓人感到孤獨，尤其是在這個社群媒體的時代。在臉書和 IG 這些地方，你可能會看到很多人開心的照片，但你永遠不知道他們的生活中有什麼正在發生。事實上，有些名人患有社交焦慮症，並且也公開談論他們與之對抗的經驗。顯見這樣的挑戰並不如想像中罕見。

Naomi Osaka，這位以擊敗 Serena Williams 而聞名的日本知名網球選手，一直在努力面對社交焦慮。她雖然身為網球偶像，但為了保護自己的心理健康，不得不在法網公開賽期間取消媒體採訪。Osaka 坦承自己有憂鬱症且性格內向。錦標賽期間，她必須在戴上頭罩式耳機來應對社交焦慮。消息公布後，她得到了其他運動員的支持。

著名女演員 Kim Basinger 也在努力對抗社交焦慮。她常常感到極度恐懼，甚至當她被要求在課堂上朗讀時，還一度精神崩潰。Basinger 在奧斯卡得獎演說中掙扎地尋找適當的字詞，並試圖討論她的焦慮和恐慌發作。心理治療有所幫助，但挑戰依然存在。

從這些受到眾人喜愛的名人身上，可以看到社交焦慮是正常的。你可以在需要時尋求協助。而透過經驗的分享，你也可能幫助到面臨類似挑戰的其他人。請記得，談論自己的感受並不是什麼問題，支持永遠都在你身邊。

1. 這篇文章最可能出現在什麼地方？
   (A) 以當代藝術為主題的廣告。
   (B) 美術館的網站。
   (C) 談論奧斯卡獎得主的小冊子。
   (D) 提升心理健康意識的運動。

2. 根據本文，Naomi Osaka 在錦標賽期間如何處理社交焦慮症？
   (A) 取消媒體採訪。
   (B) 避免使用社群媒體。
   (C) 參加心理療程。
   (D) 戴上頭罩式耳機。

3. 關於 Kim Basinger 社交焦慮的經驗，下列何者可從本文推論得知？
   (A) 她在進行奧斯卡得獎演說時，不曾遇到任何挑戰。
   (B) 心理治療完全解決了她的社交焦慮問題。
   (C) 她因為極度的恐懼，很難在課堂上朗讀。
   (D) 她輕易地克服了自己的焦慮症。

4. 作者在文中的「introverted nature」是什麼意思？
   (A) 害羞拘謹的個性。
   (B) 外向且擅於社交的朋友。
   (C) 對運動的興趣缺乏。
   (D) 對媒體採訪的偏愛。

5. 第二段的「cope with」最有可能是什麼意思？
   (A) 掙扎。 **(B) 處理。** (C) 避免。 (D) 忽視。

> **Try it!**
> 1. celebrities　2. struggle　3. breakdown
> 4. shared　5. support

---

celebrity n. 名人　　　　　struggle v. 努力；掙扎　　　icon n. 偶像；圖示
share v. 分享　　　　　　　breakdown n. (精神) 崩潰　　uncommon adj. 不尋常的
support n. 支持　　　　　　mental adj. 心理的　　　　　athlete n. 運動員

你的思考方式就代表你的一切
Your Thinking Is Your Everything

成功人士的思考方式究竟與其他人有何不同?是什麼驅使他們邁向成功之路?訪談與研究顯示,成功人士的確有一些共同的特質。

首先,成功者鮮少會輕視失敗者,他們相信如果他或她持續努力嘗試,也終有成功的一天;成功者也相信他們的未來是由自己一手打造;他們接受並非人生中的每件事都在自己的掌控之中,但他們可以選擇自己思考的方式和作為。

讓成功者與眾不同的最重要因素 ,可能就是——他們活在強烈的使命感當中。他們也許會花很長一段時間尋找適合他們的工作 ,但他們需要去做他們所認定的工作。活得有目的對他們而言無比重要;此外,成功人士絕不輕易放棄,一旦決心得到某樣東西,他們就會準備好接受一路上所有的挑戰。

1. 本文主要是關於 _____ 。
   (A) **是什麼導致人們成功**
   (B) 成功人士選擇哪些工作
   (C) 成功人士如何對待失敗者
   (D) 成功人士如何讓每件事都在他們掌控之中
   → 選項 B 太廣義,選項 C 太狹隘,選項 D 意思錯誤。

2. 成功人士為何鮮少輕視失敗者?
   (A) 因為他們自己以前也曾失敗過。
   (B) 因為他們可以幫助他或她打造未來。
   (C) 因為他們可以幫助他或她掌控每件事。
   (D) **因為他們相信他或她將來有一天也會成功。**

3. 成功人士之所以和一般人不同 , 主要是因為他們 _____ 。
   (A) 努力工作的信念
   (B) **強烈的使命感**
   (C) 強烈的責任感
   (D) 對自己的信念

4. 下列有關成功人士的敘述,何者不正確?
   (A) 只要是他們打算要做的事,他們就絕不會放棄。
   (B) 他們花費大量時間尋找生命的目標。
   (C) 他們有某些共同特質,而這些特質讓他們與其他人不同。
   (D) **遇上挑戰時,他們總改變心意。**

5. 在最後一段中出現的片語 「mean the world to someone」意思是 _____ 。
   (A) **對某人而言很重要**
   (B) 非常著名或受歡迎
   (C) 有豐富的人生經驗
   (D) 讓某人印象非常深刻

Try it!
1. To begin with
2. take on
3. look down on
4. a couple of
5. in common

to begin with 首先	drive v. 驅使	set someone apart 使某人不同
take on 承擔	seldom adv. 很少地	sense n. 意識;觀念
look down on 看輕	fail v. 失敗	look for 尋找
a couple of 幾個	accept v. 接受	quitter n. 輕易放棄者
in common 共通的	control n. 控制	challenge n. 挑戰

從害羞到廣受歡迎
From Shyness to Social Success

親愛的賈斯汀，

　　害羞可能是你問題的起因。 由於你覺得自己不夠有吸引力， 所以可能會過於害羞而不敢認識新朋友。 我有一些訣竅可以幫助你建立自信。你需要做的事只有一件，那就是向你的同學證明你其實是個很棒的人。

　　該採取的第一個步驟就是微笑。 一個真誠的笑容清楚表明了你交友的意願。 要經常這麼做，直到你的同學習慣它，並以笑容回應。

　　接下來，試著與你周遭的人談話。以非正式的閒談做為開始，可以聊些周遭剛發生過的事。一天中最恰當的時機就是在課間休息或午餐休息時，在你同學不忙的時候接近他們。在人們獨處的時候，開始一段談話會比較容易。

　　瞭解一個人需要時間，同樣地，要找到一個能與真實的你自在相處的人，也需要時間。

　　持續地去實踐這些訣竅，然後有一天，你就會發現自己從來就不曾這麼有魅力過。

馬爾文大叔

1. 本文主要是關於 ＿＿＿＿＿ 。
　(A) 如何變得有吸引力 (B) 如何交新朋友
　(C) 如何變成很棒的人 **(D) 如何克服害羞問題**
2. 本文有可能出現在 ＿＿＿＿＿ 。
　(A) 醫學期刊　　　　(B) 科學期刊
　(C) 設計雜誌　　　　**(D) 報紙專欄**
3. 為什麼賈斯汀見到陌生人會害羞？
　(A) 因為他過於自信。
　(B) 因為他不夠真誠。
　(C) 因為他不願意交朋友。

　(D) 因為他認為他不夠有吸引力。
4. 馬爾文建議賈斯汀做什麼？
　(A) 保持笑容。　　　(B) 建立自信。
　(C) 試著建立對話。　**(D) 以上皆是。**
5. 以下何者不正確？
　(A) 要瞭解一個人得花上一些時間。
　(B) 在人們忙碌的時候比較容易開啟一段對話。
　(C) 面帶微笑表示一個人樂意交朋友。
　(D) 以周遭的事物來開始一段對話是個好主意。

🎯 Try it!

1. confidence　　　　2. approached
3. surroundings　　　4. became used to
5. attractive

---

confidence	n.	信心	shy	adj.	害羞的	chat	n.	聊天
approach	v.	接近	cause	n.	原因	immediate	adj.	目前的
surroundings	n.	環境	tip	n.	訣竅	break	n.	休息時間
become used to		變得習慣	sincere	adj.	真誠的	strike up		開始建立
attractive	adj.	有吸引力的	willingness	n.	意願	similarly	adv.	同樣地

14 多媒體資訊機
Kiosks

　　自助多媒體資訊機可以幫助個人和企業處理簡單的任務。它們能夠快速解決許多問題並提供多種形式的便利。這些機器已經存在很久了。它們最初是簡單的自動販賣機，後來發展成為今日的互動式多媒體資訊機。

　　多媒體資訊機可以減少顧客和員工之間的交談量。而且它們很容易保持清潔。這在新冠肺炎危機期間和之後很重要，因為人們想要安全的處理方式。有些多媒體資訊機甚至不需要觸摸即可運行，例如使用智慧型手機代碼購買商品。這稱為非接觸式體驗。

　　多媒體資訊機對於難以找到員工的企業也有好處。它們使用簡單，因此企業無需大量員工即可提供良好的服務。即使幫助那些無法使用多媒體資訊機的人，也比讓專人幫助每位顧客所需的人員更少。

　　對客戶來說，自助式多媒體資訊機的一大好處是可以縮短等待時間。你可以在自助式多媒體資訊機上快速選擇你想要的商品，而不用排隊等候。許多商店的顧客等待服務的時間縮短了40%。如果你知道自己想要什麼，使用自助式多媒體資訊機既快速又可以保持排隊隊伍快速前進。

　　無論你從事什麼類型的業務，自助多媒體資訊機都可以讓事情變得更好。如果使用得當，它們可以幫助企業省錢，幫助客戶節省時間，並使每個人的事情變得更輕鬆！

1. 第三段主要講了什麼內容？
   (A) **企業為何使用自助式多媒體資訊機。**
   (B) 企業為何不喜歡自助式多媒體資訊機。
   (C) 企業用什麼來取代自助式多媒體資訊機。
   (D) 自助式多媒體資訊機從什麼時候開始為企業提供協助。

2. 根據本文，為什麼自助式多媒體資訊機在新冠肺炎期間很重要？
   (A) 因為他們可以用更少的員工提供良好的服務。
   (B) 因為他們可以避免等待時間。
   (C) **因為它們可以提供非接觸式體驗。**
   (D) 因為他們可以收集有關客戶習慣的資料。

3. 這篇文章的目的為何？
   (A) 批評自助式多媒體資訊機的使用。
   (B) 描述清潔企業如何使用多媒體資訊機。
   (C) 讓讀者了解多媒體資訊機的歷史。
   (D) **證明自助式多媒體資訊機的好處。**

4. 第三段的「staff」一詞最有可能是什麼意思？
   (A) 顧客。　(B) **員工。**　(C) 機器。　(D) 商店。

5. 下列何者最能描述作者對自助式多媒體資訊機的態度？
   (A) 負面的。　　　　(B) **積極的。**
   (C) 懷疑的。　　　　(D) 保守的。

 Try it!

1. interactive　2. touchless　3. decrease
4. tasks　　　5. convenience

---

task n. 任務　　　　touchless adj. 無接觸的　　reduce v. 減少
convenience n. 便利　decrease n. 下降　　　　efficient adj. 有效率的
interactive adj. 互動的　develop into 演變　　　assist v. 幫助

15 小心身後
Watch Out Behind You

　　一所位於倫敦近郊的學校允許學生在下午時間進城，不過有個條件：他們必須在晚上六點前回來。一天下午，鮑伯到市中心去看了場電影，當他回到學校的時候，校門已經關閉了。他繞到校園的另一頭，希望能從後門進去，不幸地，後門也關了，然後他看到了在幾呎遠的地方，有一扇窗戶敞開著。

　　那扇窗戶通往校長的辦公室。鮑伯把頭探進房間，心裡想：「這裡連個鬼影子都沒有。」然後他很快地爬進房間，就在這時候，他聽到一個熟悉的聲音，所以躲到辦公椅的後面。原來走進來的是校長。校長坐到椅子上，看了一小時的書。最後，校長從椅子上站起來，朝著門的方向走去。「呼！好險！」鮑伯想著。正當他要起身離開的時候，校長朝著椅子的方向說：「可以請你把燈關掉嗎？」

1. 學生可以在下午時間進城，只要他們 _____。
   (A) 是去那裡看電影
   (B) 在晚上六點前回到學校
   (C) 在離開前把燈關掉
   (D) 從後門進校園

2. 鮑伯到市中心的目的為何？
   (A) 購物。　　　　　**(B) 看電影。**
   (C) 見朋友。　　　　(D) 見校長。

3. 為何鮑伯要爬進校長的辦公室？
   (A) 因為它的門是開著的。
   (B) 因為學校大門關閉了。
   (C) 因為房間裡擠滿了人。

(D) 因為房間裡燈火通明。

4. 最後一段中，「There is not a soul in here」是什麼意思？
   (A) 這房間鬧鬼。
   (B) 這房間很暗。
   (C) 這房間裡沒人。
   (D) 房間裡很冷。
   → 這裡的 soul 表示「人」。

5. 這個故事的笑點是什麼？
   (A) 校長以為椅子會說話。
   (B) 校長不知道鮑伯在辦公室裡。
   (C) 校長自己不知道門是關著的。
   (D) 校長知道鮑伯在他辦公室裡，而且還以輕鬆的方式說話。

> 💡 **Try it!**
>
> 1. leads to　　2. familiar　　3. downtown
> 4. at last　　5. allowed

lead to　通往	suburban　adj.　近郊的	principal　n.　校長
familiar　adj.　熟悉的	condition　n.　條件	poke　v.　向前伸
downtown　n.　市中心	gate　n.　大門	voice　n.　聲音
at last　最終	campus　n.　校園	towards　adv.　朝向
allow　v.　允許	wide open　敞開的	turn off　關上 (開關)

16 符號比文字更有力
Signs Speak Louder Than Words

你用文字交談和書寫，而訊息被傳送及接收。人們利用文字溝通已如此之久，但不使用文字的溝通又是如何？

面露微笑，你告訴人們你的心情正好。你哭泣，別人就曉得你情緒低落。如果你舉起你的手，老師會給你機會發言或詢問。在某些文化中，你搖頭表示不要，點頭表示贊同。

這些並非傳達訊息僅有的工具，符號在這方面可能比文字更為有力。比方說，當紅燈亮起，駕駛人就該停下車來，否則警官會要求他們把車停到路邊。牆上的一個標誌可能會讓吸煙者將香煙捻熄，不然就會遭罰款處分。或許這是你第一次瞭解到這些符號在對你說話，但除此之外呢？

藝術家以繪畫來表達他們對夕陽的喜愛，人們用圖畫來呈現對戰爭的憤怒及愛情的甘苦，其他類似的例子可說是不勝枚舉。

1. 本文主要是關於 _____。
  (A) 符號的作用為何
  (B) 人們如何利用手勢溝通
  (C) 人們如何用文字表達自己
  (D) 人們如何在不使用文字的狀況下，表達他們的意見或情感
  → 選項 A、B 較狹隘，不足以代表本文主旨。
2. 人們可用下列何者溝通？
  (A) 文字。　　　　(B) 肢體語言。
  (C) 臉部表情。　　(D) 以上皆是。
  → 第二段提到 smile 屬 facial expressions，舉手、搖頭和點頭則屬 gestures 或廣義的 body language。
3. 一個人舉起手來表示他或她 _____。
  (A) 心情很好　　　(B) 覺得情緒低落
  (C) 有問題要問　　(D) 贊同
4. 看到紅燈亮起時，駕駛人可能會 _____。
  (A) 靠邊停車　　　(B) 加速
  (C) 逐漸加速　　　(D) 停下來
  → pull over 表「把 (車) 開到路邊」，speed up 和 pick up speed 均表「加速」。
5. 下列何者不是「不以文字溝通」的範例？
  (A) 畫作。　　　　(C) 音樂。
  (C) 書籍。　　　　(D) 以上皆是。

Try it!
1. message　　2. in a good mood
3. put out　　4. pull over
5. communicate

message n. 訊息	receive v. 接收	cigarette n. 香菸
in a good mood 心情很好	raise v. 舉起	fine v. 處以罰款
put out 熄滅	shake v. 搖動	realize v. 了解
pull over 將車開至路邊停下	nod v. 點頭	sunshine n. 陽光
communicate v. 溝通	sign n. 符號	bittersweetness n. 苦樂參半

17 南韓的 MBTI 風潮
The MBTI Fad in South Korea

　　Myers-Briggs 類型指標 (MBTI) 是 1943 年制定的關於人格的測驗。它觀察四件事：你比較外向，還是比較安靜；你專注於事實，還是專注於可能性；你做決定是用頭腦，還是看心情；你喜歡擬定計畫，還是臨場應變。這個測驗會將你分到 16 組人格的其中一個。

　　在南韓，很多人非常喜歡 MBTI。他們認為這可以幫助他們找到合適的工作或伴侶。企業用它來選擇僱用人員和工作夥伴。甚至一些約會應用程式也用它來幫人配對。但有一些批評者表示 MBTI 並不可靠。他們認為它並不能精確衡量人們的個性。他們也擔心在工作場所使用它可能並不公平。舉例來說，老闆可能會挑選外向的人而非安靜的人，即使安靜的人工作做得更好。

　　儘管有這些問題，許多南韓人仍然喜歡 MBTI。有些人甚至用它來猜測未來的走向。在一齣 2018 年的電視劇中，MBTI 便被用來尋找罪犯。背後的想法是，某些人格類型更有可能犯下某些罪行。但專家表示這個想法相當不妥。他們爭論說，在預測你是否會犯罪時，成長方式和居住地點等因素比你的個性更重要。

　　由於觀看人數不多，該劇播出一季後就被取消了。但會做出這樣的節目這件事，充分顯示了 MBTI 對韓國社會的影響有多大。這究竟是好是壞，依然有待討論。

1. 這篇文章的主要目的為何？
  (A) 推廣 MBTI 在職場的使用。
  (B) 批評南韓的約會應用程式。
  (C) 討論 **MBTI** 的不可靠之處。
  (D) 支持取消不受歡迎的電視劇。

2. 這篇文章是用什麼方式組織架構的？
  (A) 依時間先後。
  (B) 列出優點和缺點。
  (C) 依因果關係。
  (D) 比較不同的人格測驗。

3. 南韓企業使用 MBTI 的主要原因為何？
  (A) 用來決定僱用人員和工作夥伴。
  (B) 用來幫員工和適合的對象配對。
  (C) 用來預測未來的工作表現。
  (D) 用來批評聘僱程序。

4. 哪裡最有可能找到關於 MBTI 對南韓社會衝擊的資訊？
  (A) 電視節目腳本。
  (B) 談論人格測驗的歷史書。
  (C) 給在南韓觀光客的導覽手冊。
  (D) 南韓的報紙文章。

5. 關於 MBTI 對南韓社會的影響，作者有著怎樣的感受？
  (A) 興奮。
  (B) 中立。
  (C) 批判。
  (D) 困惑。

Try it!

1. outgoing 2. suitable 3. predict
4. measure 5. reliable

---

outgoing　adj.　外向的
predict　v.　預測
reliable　adj.　可靠的

suitable　adj.　適合的
measure　v.　測量，衡量
possibility　n.　可能性

critic　n.　批評家，評論家
criminal　n.　罪犯
affect　v.　影響

18 小心你的心境！
Mind Your Mind!

很久很久以前，在一個遙遠的小村莊裡，有一棟千鏡之屋。有一天，有一隻快樂的狗來到這座屋子，牠以輕快的腳步跑上台階，在入口處，牠抱著濃厚的興趣打量裡面。令牠驚訝的是，牠發現有其他一千隻快樂的狗望著牠。更奇妙的是，當牠微笑時，牠們全都以微笑回報。離開這棟屋子時，牠很滿足，並認為自己以後應該常來這裡。

不久後，一隻憂鬱的狗來到同一座屋子，但情況完全不同。不像那隻快樂的狗，牠彷彿心事重重地拖著沈重腳步爬上樓梯。當牠望進屋子裡時，看到的是一千隻兇猛的狗，牠開始憤怒地朝牠們吠叫，結果只害自己嚇得要命，因為有一千隻狗對牠報以咆哮怒吼。當牠離開屋子時，牠告訴自己，以後再也不要到這個可怕的地方來了。

這個故事告訴我們：隨著自己不同的心境，眼中他人的樣貌也會不同。所以，你想看到哪一種臉龐呢？決定權完全在你身上。

1. 這個故事的主旨是 _____ 。
   (A) 快樂的狗有比較多同伴
   (B) 面對危險時應保持冷靜
   (C) 若一隻狗朝其他狗吠叫，牠們會以咆哮怒吼回應
   (D) 我們的心境會影響我們感知周遭人事物的方式

2. 為何快樂的狗發現有其他一千隻狗對牠報以微笑？
   (A) 因為牠常去拜訪牠們。

(B) 因為這是牠們迎接客人的方式。
   (C) 因為牠在鏡子裡看到自己的倒映。
   (D) 因為牠抱著濃厚興趣察看這座屋子。
   → 答題關鍵 reflection 表示「(鏡中) 倒映」。

3. 以下何者未被用來描述憂鬱的狗？
   (A) 兇猛的。　　　　　　**(B) 快樂的。**
   (C) 憤怒的。　　　　　　(D) 心事重重的。
   → 「had something on his mind」表示「若有所思」，意思相當於 lost in thought。

4. 第二段中的「blue」意指 _____ 。
   (A) 憂鬱的 (B) 憤怒的 (C) 愉悅的 (D) 滿意的
   → 於此 blue 表示「沮喪的，憂鬱的」。

5. 在故事中，作者將我們的心境比做 _____ 。
   (A) 狗　　　　　　　　　**(B) 鏡子**
   (C) 一棟房屋　　　　　　(D) 一座遙遠的小村莊

🔦 Try it!
1. Check out　　　　　2. terror
3. Once upon a time　　4. enthusiasm
5. located

---

check out　查看	remote　adj.　遙遠的	gaze　v.　注視
terror　n.　懼怕	mirror　n.　鏡子	fierce　adj.　兇猛的
once upon a time　很久以前	stair　n.　樓梯	bark　v.　吠叫
enthusiasm　n.　熱忱	entrance　n.　入口	growl　v.　低聲吠叫
locate　v.　坐落於	amazement　n.　驚訝	totally　adv.　完全地

19 靈動的職業生涯
An Animated Career

孩提時代的宮崎駿很喜歡閱讀和畫畫。1963 年自大學畢業後，他開始在東映動畫公司工作。1984 年，《風之谷》躍上日本的大銀幕。這是一部由宮崎駿創作的漫畫改編而來的動畫。這部動畫電影大獲成功，讓宮崎駿能夠組成自己的動畫公司，也就是吉卜力工作室。

　　1988 年的《龍貓》是宮崎駿最受歡迎的動畫電影之一，孩童和年輕人都非常喜愛這部片。故事是關於兩姊妹和一隻名叫「豆豆龍」貓之間的溫馨友情。片中的「貓巴士」，亦即一隻變成巴士的貓，以及煤炭精靈，一種住在黑暗中的塵埃生物，都既有趣又可愛。2001 年的《神隱少女》更是一部比《龍貓》還受歡迎的作品。

　　宮崎駿的電影與眾不同之處就在於創意。一座位於雲端的王國或會移動的城堡捕捉住人們的想像力，一些魔法元素也使這些故事更添魅力；被施下咒語的人會變成豬、鳥、龍等生物。有趣的情節再加上多樣化的角色，我們可以說，宮崎駿的電影將會歷久不衰。

1. 本篇文章主要是關於 ＿＿＿＿＿＿ 。
   (A) 宮崎駿的一生
   (B) 宮崎駿的童年
   (C) 宮崎駿作品的成功
   (D) 宮崎駿電影中的魔法
2. 宮崎駿在 ＿＿＿＿＿ 年從大學畢業。
   (A) 1936　(B) 1948　**(C) 1963**　(D) 1984
3. 在 ＿＿＿＿＿ 上映後，宮崎駿開設了自己的動畫公司。
   (A)《魔法公主》　　(B)《龍貓》
   (C)《神隱少女》　　**(D)《風之谷》**
4. 出現在第一段的詞語「big screen」意指 ＿＿＿＿＿ 。
   (A) 電影院
   (B) 電視機前面的平坦表面
   (C) 阻止蚊蟲在外的金屬或塑膠網
   (D) 遮住視線的東西
   → screen 可以表示「(電視的) 螢光幕」、「紗窗，紗門」、「幕，簾」，於此表示「大銀幕 (指電影院)」。
5. 下列敘述何者正確？
   (A) 宮崎駿電影與眾不同的原因在於一些魔法元素。
   (B)《神隱少女》甚至比《龍貓》還受歡迎。
   (C)《龍貓》是關於兩姊妹和煤炭精靈的友情故事。
   (D)《風之谷》改編自兩姊妹畫的漫畫書。

Try it!
1. imagination 2. creative 3. come out
4. friendship 5. captured

imagination n. 想像力　animated adj. 動畫的　creature n. 生物
creative adj. 創意的　adult n. 成人　kingdom n. 王國
come out 出版　soot n. 煤灰　castle n. 城堡
friendship n. 友誼　sprite n. 精靈　spell n. 咒語
capture v. 捕捉　dust n. 灰塵　dragon n. 龍

19

20 愛的力量
The Power of Love

「愛征服一切」這句話可能有一個新的解讀方式。以下是有關一對母子之間的真實故事，發生的地點在澳洲內陸。

某天，一位名叫麗茲的單親媽媽正在洗衣服，而她五歲的兒子艾瑞克獨自在後院玩耍。

突然，麗茲聽來自後院的哭喊聲。她慌忙地衝出後門，結果發現有條大蛇正要把她兒子給吞了！那嚇壞了麗茲，但是，她當場就決定要將她兒子安全救回。麗茲完全沒意識到情況有多危險，就抓起一把鋤頭，奮力地攻擊那隻怪物。

麗茲狂亂地、一次又一次地攻擊那條蛇。然而，艾瑞克的呼吸只是逐漸變弱，而這讓麗茲幾近瘋狂——她撲向那條蛇，張開她的嘴巴，咬住牠的身體。

一看到怪物身上被自己咬的傷口，麗茲就再次拿起鋤頭，用她全身的力氣攻擊那個傷口。那蛇被傷的如此嚴重，以致牠必須要放走男孩才能逃跑。那怪物從沒想過，人咬可以造成這麼大的傷害！而扭轉情勢的，正是母親的愛。

1. 本文主要是關於_____。
   (A) **母愛有多偉大**
   (B) 蛇可能有多危險
   (C) 人咬可以造成多大的傷害
   (D) 在緊急狀況中，人可以做些什麼
2. 在第一段中「twist」意思為何？
   (A) 馬路上的一個急轉彎。
   (B) **意義的改變。**
   (C) 預料之外的客人。

(D) 用雙手擰轉某物的動作。
→ twist 可以表示「轉彎處」、「彎曲」、「意想不到的轉折或發展」，但於此表示「其他的解釋；轉折」。

3. 當艾瑞克在後院玩耍的時候，發生了什麼事？
   (A) 他試圖去咬一條蛇。
   (B) **他被一條蛇攻擊。**
   (C) 一條蛇試圖要吞下他媽媽。
   (D) 他抓起鋤頭，用力砍打一條蛇。
4. 那條蛇為何放走了男孩？
   (A) 因為牠怕鋤頭。
   (B) **因為牠受了重傷。**
   (C) 因為牠被男孩咬了。
   (D) 因為牠的呼吸變得愈來愈弱。
5. 以下敘述何者正確？
   (A) **那男孩並沒有跟他父親住在一起。**
   (B) 麗茲咬那條蛇是因為她瘋了。
   (C) 諺語「愛征服一切」並不適用於這個故事。
   (D) 麗茲先以槍傷了那條蛇，之後再用全身的力量咬牠。
   → 從用字 a single mother「單親媽媽」可得知，選項 A 是正確的。

> **Try it!**
> 1. scared   2. conquer
> 3. then and there   4. grabbed
> 5. ate up

---

scare v. 使驚嚇	twist n. 轉折	hoe n. 鋤頭
conquer v. 征服	single adj. 單身的	frantically adv. 瘋狂地
then and there 當場	do the laundry 洗衣服	wound n. 傷口
grab v. 抓住	backyard n. 後院	strength n. 力量
eat up 吃完	unaware adj. 未察覺的	occur v. 發生

口香糖的由來
Where Chewing Gum Began

口香糖的歷史十分悠久。瑞典科學家發現一塊能追溯到九千年前的口香糖，在這塊口香糖上，甚至還能看到一名青少年的齒痕！然而，現代的口香糖直到約 1870 年才出現。湯瑪斯·亞當斯原本為了想做橡膠，從墨西哥的一棵樹中取出一些液體，最後卻發現製作口香糖的方法。後來，他所製作的口香糖造成轟動，於是愈來愈多人開始投入口香糖業。

1892 年，威廉·瑞格理開始經營口香糖事業。他所生產的口香糖受到美國人歡迎，為他帶來龐大財富。今日，箭牌公司的口香糖生產量達到每年十億條。在美國，每人一年平均吃掉 170 到 180 片口香糖。

然而，有些人並不喜歡這種情況，包括自由女神像的工作人員。有待清理的口香糖多到他們不得不在雕像旁設置垃圾桶，上面有塊告示牌寫著：「把口香糖放在這裡」的牌子。但人們卻直接照字面所說的做——把口香糖黏在那塊牌子上！

1. 本篇文章主要是關於 _____ 。
   (A) 口香糖的歷史　　(B) 口香糖的生產
   (C) 口香糖業界　　(D) 發明口香糖的人
2. 現代的口香糖可追溯至約 _____ 年前。
   (A) 140　　(B) 180　　(C) 1,870　　(D) 9,000
3. 誰發明了口香糖？
   (A) 一名墨西哥人。　　**(B) 湯瑪斯·亞當斯。**
   (C) 威廉·瑞格理。　　(D) 瑞典科學家們。

4. 在 _____ 年，威廉·瑞格理開始經營口香糖事業。
   (A) 1870　　(B) 1829　　**(C) 1892**　　(D) 1982
5. 下列敘述何者正確？
   (A) 第一段中「hit」意指失敗。
   (B) 威廉·瑞格理靠生產橡膠而獲得龐大財富。
   (C) 在美國，平均每人每年吃掉 170 到 180 片口香糖。
   (D) 在自由女神像旁，人們被要求把口香糖黏在一個垃圾桶的告示牌上。
   → hit 於此表示「成功而風行一時的事物」。

Try it!
1. discover　　2. consuming
3. made a fortune　　4. production
5. traced back

---

discover v. 發現	history n. 歷史	stick n. 條 (狀)
consume v. 吃；喝	chew v. 咀嚼	situation n. 情況
make a fortune 發財	visible adj. 可見的	statue n. 雕像
production n. 產量	exist v. 存在	liberty n. 自由
trace back 回溯	rubber n. 橡膠	literally adv. 照字面上地

對許多人來說，如「講重點」、「說實話」或「就去做吧」是非常美式的表達方式。這種直接的美式風格支持對的事物，但也許會嚇到來自世界其他地區的人。

例如，美國小孩不怕質疑父母或老師的想法，辦公室職員被鼓勵在經理面前勇於表達自己的意見。然而，某些文化認為尊重長者和在位者很重要，他們偏好用暗示的方式表達自己，以免傷害到別人的感覺。

美式風格的另一個特質是競爭。它驅使人們「懷抱夢想」、「使夢想成真」，並成為「箇中翹楚」。但美國人可能會給人咄咄逼人或不易共事的感覺。

美國人喜歡快且實際的東西，喜歡不說廢話、不浪費時間的人。但近來歐洲興起一種「慢活運動」，重新思考過去做事的方式。

雖然不可能消弭所有歧異，但大部分外國人仍覺得美國人是友善、充滿活力和有創意的。這也是世界各地的人前往美國尋找新生活和新機會的原因。

1. 這篇文章主要是關於 _____ 。
   (**A**) **美國精神**
   (B) 美國習俗
   (C) 美國人普遍的表達方式
   (D) 美國小孩的態度問題
2. 第一段的片語「stand up for」意指 _____ 。
   (A) 容易可見　　　(B) 抗拒某人
   (C) 站穩腳步　　　(**D**) **支持某事**

→ stand up 表示「支持」。
3. 人們用暗示的方式是因為害怕 _____ 。
   (A) 懷抱夢想　　　(B) 成為箇中翹楚
   (C) 表達自我　　　(**D**) **傷害別人的感覺**
4. 下列何者是美式風格的特質？
   (A) 競爭。　　　　(B) 直接。
   (C) 快且實際。　　(**D**) **以上皆是。**
5. 下列敘述何者正確？
   (A) 近來美國興起「慢活運動」。
   (**B**) **「講重點」的表達方式顯示美國人喜歡直接了當。**
   (C) 競爭讓美國人容易與人相處。
   (D) 大多數外國人在消弭和美國人之間的歧異後，認為美國人很友善。

Try it!
1. competition　2. speak up　　3. feature
4. direct　　　5. hint

competition n. 競爭	style n. 風格	type n. 類別
speak up 大膽說出	hurt v. 傷害	guy n. 人
feature n. 特色	come across as 留下印象	waste v. 浪費
direct adj. 直接的	pushy adj. 強勢的	rise n. 興起
hint n. 暗示	workable adj. 實際可行的	foreigner n. 外國人

一路順風
Travel Your Way

　　沒有旅行的現代生活是難以想像的 ，而旅行最快的方式就是搭飛機。今日，你可以訂張機票，並享受單日的行程，而這樣的行程在一個世紀之前 ，可能要花上多於一個月的時間才能完成。

　　搭火車旅行花的時間較長 ，但也有它的好處。它讓你可以仔細觀察你旅程行經的國家。現代的火車提供舒適的座位以及餐飲區 ，即使是再長的旅程，也會讓人覺得短暫。

　　有些人喜歡由海路旅行 ，而遠洋渡輪的歷史也已相當久遠 。它們通常以五星級住宿和精緻食物為特色。此外，甲板上多種刺激的活動，你也絕不會感到無聊。

　　其他人喜歡搭乘汽車旅行 。 你可以依據自己的行程及計畫行動，比方說，在一天內你可以隨性地走個 2 哩或 50 哩，甚至長達 200 哩，而且你可以停在任何你想停留之處 ： 像是在森林裡呼吸一些新鮮空氣 、 在海邊游泳或待在旅館休息一下 。 那就是為什麼比較多人喜歡開車旅遊玩樂，而生意人由於沒太多時間，會選擇搭火車或飛機的原因了。

1. 本文主要是關於 _____ 。
　(**A**) 旅行　　　　　(B) 現代生活
　(C) 現代火車　　　(D) 遠洋渡輪
　→ 選項 B 太廣義，選項 C、D 太狹隘。
2. 如果你是個時間不多的生意人 ，你可能會利用 _____ 旅行。
　(A) 火車　　　　　(B) 腳踏車
　(**C**) 飛機　　　　　(D) 遠洋渡輪

3. 搭火車旅行的優點為何？
　(A) 你可以節省很多時間。
　(B) 你可以停在任何你想停的地方。
　(C) 你可以享受甲板上許多刺激的活動。
　(**D**) 你可以仔細觀察你旅遊行經的國家。
4. 自行開車旅行的優點為何？
　(A) 它是最快的旅行方式。
　(B) 你會有舒適的座位以及餐飲區。
　(C) 你會有五星級的住宿以及精緻的食物。
　(**D**) 你可以根據自己的計畫及行程旅行。
5. 以下敘述何者正確？
　(A) 現代火車以五星級住宿和精緻的食物為特色。
　(B) 搭火車旅遊所花的時間較長，而且一點好處都沒有。
　(**C**) 現今一天能抵達的旅程在過去可能要花上一個月或更久的時間。
　(D) 由於有舒適的座位以及餐飲區，在飛機上最長的旅程也可能讓人感覺短暫。

Try it!
1. complete　　2. journey　　3. opted for
4. used to　　5. advantages

complete　v.　完成
journey　n.　旅程
opt for　選擇
used to　過去習慣
advantage　n.　好處

century　n.　世紀
liner　n.　郵輪
feature　v.　以…為特色
lodging　n.　住房
deck　n.　甲板

schedule　n.　行程表
wherever　adv.　不論何處
woods　n.　樹林
beach　n.　海灘
opt for　傾向於

麵條哪裡來？
Where Did Noodles Come From?

　　麵條在世界各地許多國家都很受歡迎，但許多年來，人們對於麵條的確切起源地爭論不休。有些人認為，義大利人發明麵條，再經由絲路帶到中國。還有些人認為，阿拉伯人發明了麵條，再分享給義大利和中國。許多中國人則聲稱，麵條由中國人所發明，再經由絲路傳到中東、義大利和世界各地。

　　然而，最近在中國的一項發現，有可能為這場爭議劃下句點。在一座位於黃河附近的考古遺跡中，發現了世界上最早的麵條，這些麵條已有超過四千年歷史。不像現今的麵條，它們並非由小麥粉製成，而是由小米製成。這些黃色麵條被存放在一個被大洪水掩埋的鍋子中。根據該處一名科學家表示，這些麵條看起來像「拉麵」，一種以手拉方式製作的傳統中國麵條。

　　因此，由於在中國發現這些世上最早的麵條，我們似乎可以相當肯定地說，麵條是在該地發明，之後才透過絲路傳到世界其他地方。

1. 許多人都說他們發明了麵條，除了 _____ 以外。
(A) 中國人　(B) 阿拉伯人
(C) 義大利人　**(D) 西班牙人**
2. 麵條經由 _____ 傳至其他國家。
(A) 黃河　**(B) 絲路**
(C) 長城　(D) 阿拉伯海
3. 本篇文章的目的在於 _____。
(A) 提倡麵條是世界上最好的食物
(B) 確保中國在烹煮麵條上佔有一席之地
(C) 說明麵條起源於何處
(D) 討論為何麵條在許多地方都很受歡迎
4. 現代麵條是由 _____ 製成。
(A) 小米　(B) 糙米　**(C) 小麥粉**　(D) 玉米
5. 關於世界上最早的麵條，下列敘述何者正確？
(A) 它們在黃河附近被發現。
(B) 它們的歷史超過 40,000 年。
(C) 它們在一個位於山上的鍋子裡被發現。
(D) 他們看起來像傳統日本「拉」麵。

Try it!
1. According to　2. wheat
3. buried　4. claimed
5. debate

according to 根據　share v. 分享　unlike prep. 不像…
wheat n. 小麥　via prep. 經由　flour n. 麵粉
bury v. 掩埋　once and for all 最終地　millet n. 小米
claim v. 聲稱　archaeological adj. 考古學的　pot n. 鍋子
debate v. 爭論　site n. 場所；遺址　major adj. 嚴重的

我們去露營吧！
Let's Go Camping!

現在，露營比以往都更受歡迎。例如，在英國，過去兩年去露營的人數增加了 20%。然而，瘋露營不僅僅是在英國。在許多國家的公園、森林和山區，看到人們帶著帳篷和營火是很普遍的事。

那為什麼露營這麼受歡迎呢？原因之一是這是一種便宜的度假選擇。不需要花很多錢住飯店，還可以自己煮飯。因此，若你想省錢，露營是完美的選擇。另一個原因是它可以幫助你遠離科技。如今，我們總是使用手機，但當你露營時，你可以關掉所有智慧型手機，享受生活中簡單的事情。

但是如果你不喜歡睡在帳篷裡怎麼辦？現在出現了一種新的露營趨勢，稱為「豪華露營」。豪華露營是指你住在豪華帳篷裡，裡面有真正的床、冰箱，甚至還有電視！這基本上就像住在酒店一樣，但是是在戶外。世界各地都有豪華露營地，其中包括非洲、亞洲和南美洲的一些美麗的露營地。因此，如果你想嘗試露營，但又不想放棄居家般的舒適感，也許豪華露營適合你。

當然，露營並不適合所有人。有些人討厭睡在外面，而有些人則認為這很無聊，因為沒有什麼可做的。但如果你以前從未露營過，也許是時候嘗試一下了。你可能會發現一個新的愛好並跟上這波露營熱潮！

1. 這篇文章的目的為何？
   (A) 勸說人們不要嘗試露營。
   (B) 宣傳豪華露營的好處。
   (C) 討論露營的普及。
   (D) 將露營與其他戶外活動進行比較。

2. 作者如何開始這篇文章？
   (A) 講笑話。
   (B) 給定義。
   (C) 講故事。
   (D) 提供統計數據。

3. 根據本文，為什麼露營變得越來越流行？
   (A) 露營成為昂貴的度假選擇。
   (B) 露營可以讓人們脫離科技。
   (C) 露營提供許多飯店選擇。
   (D) 戶外露營比住飯店舒服。

4. 下列哪一項沒有被提及為某些人不喜歡露營的原因？
   (A) 他們更喜歡睡在室內。
   (B) 他們覺得露營很無聊。
   (C) 他們買不起露營設備。
   (D) 他們認為露營提供的活動較少。

5. 根據本文，以下關於豪華露營的敘述哪一項是正確的？
   (A) 在惡劣天候條件下露營。
   (B) 沒有任何科技設備的露營。
   (C) 入住豪華帳篷，享受居家般的舒適感。
   (D) 具有基本設施的傳統露營。

Try it!
1. comforts 　2. tent 　3. switch off
4. give up 　5. option

---

option n. 選擇	give up 放棄	luxury n. 豪華
tent n. 帳篷	switch off 關掉	outdoors n. 戶外
comfort n. 舒適的設施	craze n. 狂熱	discover v. 發現

26 失火了！逃命啊！
Fire! Escape!

每一年，火災都會奪走數千條人命。一場火災的起始通常毫無預警，而葬生火窟的人，通常都是因為在火災突然發生時過於害怕，以致無法做出反應。這裡有一些訣竅可以幫助你度過緊急狀況。

・一旦聞到煙味或看見火災，就立刻盡你所能大喊：「失火了！」這麼做是因為你的家人或鄰居可能正在睡覺。

・無論火苗多小，絕不要試著自行撲滅，而是要向人們尋求幫助或撥打911，告知消防人員你的所在地以及起火物品，保持冷靜並依照指示行動。

・如果你的房間充滿煙霧，就壓低身體。近地板處有較少的煙霧，表示著有更多的新鮮空氣，以及更多的逃生機會。

・在開門前先用你的手背測試門把。如果它是冰涼的，就小心地將門打開；如果它是燙的，你就得試著找另外的路出去。

・最後一項提示，起火後要儘快離開你的房屋，別停下來拿任何東西。火勢蔓延的速度將超乎你的想像。

1. 本文主要是關於＿＿＿＿＿。
  (A) 火勢延燒能有多迅速
  (B) 如何自行撲滅火災的訣竅
  (C) 如何逃出失火的房子
  (D) 如何在火災中自保的訣竅
  → 選項 A 與主題無關，選項 B 意思錯誤，選項 C 意思太狹隘。

2. 在看到起火或聞到煙味時，人們應該做什麼？
  (A) 大叫「失火了！」 (B) 打 911 報案。
  (C) 保持冷靜。 **(D) 以上皆是。**

3. 在找路逃出失火房屋時，應該＿＿＿＿＿。
  (A) 在開門後測試門把
  (B) 在開門前小心地觸碰門把
  (C) 在離開前收拾所有個人財物
  (D) 在開門前緊握住門把

4. 在房間充滿煙霧時，人們應該要把身體壓低，因為＿＿＿＿＿。
  (A) 門把是燙的
  (B) 在近地板處有較多的煙霧
  (C) 在近地板處有較少的新鮮空氣
  (D) 可以看到要前往的方向

5. 為何應該儘快逃出著火的房子？
  (A) 因為門把會變得非常燙。
  (B) 因為火勢可能擴展得非常迅速。
  (C) 因為他或她通常會因為太害怕而無法做出反應。
  (D) 因為他或她的家人和鄰居可能在睡覺。

 Try it!

1. emergency 2. is full of 3. imagine
4. as soon as 5. location

---

emergency n. 緊急事故	take away 奪走 (生命)	calm adj. 鎮靜的
be full of 充滿著	react v. 反應	doorknob n. 門把
imagine v. 想像	shout v. 喊叫	cool adj. 涼爽的
as soon as 一…就…	asleep adj. 睡著的	reminder n. 提醒
location n. 位置	dial v. 撥號	pick up 收拾

27 帶來勝利的植物
A Victorious Plant

接近西元一世紀末時，羅馬人和蘇格蘭人之間爆發戰爭。羅馬人在佔領英格蘭後，還想獲得蘇格蘭的控制權，一支驍勇善戰的羅馬軍隊被派往北方，每個士兵都殺氣騰騰。

由於羅馬士兵數量實在太多，蘇格蘭人似乎在打一場沒有勝算的仗。在最後一役前夕，蘇格蘭將軍對手下士兵發表談話。

「明天，我們將面臨一場非生即死的戰役。」將軍說，「現在大家好好休息，我們將戰到最後一刻！」士兵們齊聲大吼回應。

在夜色掩護下，羅馬人悄悄爬上山丘，眼看奇襲就要發動。

突然間，羅馬軍隊中發出一聲嘶吼，劃破寂靜。一名士兵因誤踩到一棵薊而傷了腳，脫口叫出聲。蘇格蘭人驚醒過來，立刻起身，宛如沒有明天般地奮勇戰鬥。沒多久，他們就打敗了羅馬軍隊。

在此之前，許多人都不知道薊這種植物。它們生長在野地，表面覆滿尖刺。很少人喜歡它，卻備受蘇格蘭人珍視，甚至還把它命為國花。

1. 這篇文章主要是關於 _____ 。
   (A) 蘇格蘭國旗
   (B) 蘇格蘭國花
   (C) 英格蘭在西元一世紀時如何被攻陷
   (D) 西元一世紀時，一場蘇格蘭人和羅馬人之間的戰爭
2. 第一段中的「capture」意指 _____ 。
   (A) 捉到一個人或一隻動物
   (B) 掌握一個地方的控制權

   (C) 使某人對某事有興趣
   (D) 拍攝或記錄某人或某事物
   → capture 於此表示「佔領」。
3. 為何蘇格蘭人似乎在打一場沒有勝算的仗？
   (A) 因為羅馬人已佔領英格蘭。
   (B) 因為羅馬士兵數量實在太多。
   (C) 因為羅馬士兵全都殺氣騰騰。
   (D) 因為最後一場戰役在夜晚降臨後才發生。
4. 為何蘇格蘭人喜愛薊？
   (A) 因為它生長在野地。
   (B) 因為它表面覆滿尖刺。
   (C) 因為許多人都不知道薊。
   (D) 因為它幫助他們打贏羅馬人。
5. 下列敘述何者正確？
   (A) 為了佔領蘇格蘭，一支驍勇善戰的羅馬軍隊被派往南方。
   (B) 在戰役前夕，蘇格蘭士兵士氣十分低迷。
   (C) 羅馬人在佔領蘇格蘭後還想佔領英格蘭。
   (D) 「Fighting a losing battle」的意思是「做一件很可能會成功的事」。
   → fight a losing battle 表示「打一場沒有把握的仗」。

Try it!
1. battle   2. Alarmed   3. broke out
4. attack   5. silence

battle n. 戰役	soldier n. 士兵	thistle n. 薊
alarm v. 使恐慌	general n. 將軍	in no time 立刻
break out (戰爭或疾病) 爆發	rest v. 休息	unknown adj. 不為人知的
attack n. 攻擊	roar v. 咆哮	sharp adj. 尖銳的
silence n. 寂靜	suddenly adv. 突然地	name v. 選定

28 經濟大蕭條的一劑強心針
The Antidepressant in the Great Depression

當紐約股市在 1929 年崩盤時，一段經濟衰敗期於焉展開。這段時間名為「經濟大蕭條」，持續十年之久，數百萬人失去工作和家園。然而，大蕭條時期並非全無好事，黑暗中仍有一些光芒。1935 年，美國總統羅斯福設立「工作改進組織」，試圖創造工作機會並改善經濟，它協助各行業的人民。

「工作改進組織」之下的方案是「聯邦作家計畫」，它對失業作家幫助特別大。在短短八年間，該計畫給予無數作家工作，像是索爾・貝羅和理查・萊特等人，日後還成為知名作家。

不過，這項計畫更以它所製作的導覽聞名。此計畫為美國四十八州製作導覽，讓人們瞭解各個城市和文化，該計畫亦討論到族群議題，因而產生各項研究，如〈紐約的義大利人〉，此外亦訪問了 2,000 名曾身為奴隸的人士。該計畫試圖透過讓人們彼此瞭解、創造全國一體的感受，在大蕭條期間提振美國人的精神。確實，在經濟大蕭條期間，並非每件事都是令人沮喪的。

1. 經濟大蕭條發生在哪段時間？
   (A) 1935 年到 1939 年。
   (B) 1929 年到 1935 年。
   (C) **1929 年到 1939 年。**
   (D) 1938 年到 1948 年。

2. 下列關於工作改進組織的敘述何者不正確？
   (A) 它由羅斯福總統設立。
   (B) 它試圖創造就業並改善經濟。
   (C) 它幫助了失業作家。
   (D) **它聘有 2,000 名員工。**

3. 最後一段中「boost」字意為何？
   (A) 驕傲地談論某事。
   (B) **將某事物提升到更高境界。**
   (C) 使某事物移到較低層次。
   (D) 到其他地方旅行。

4. 下列關於經濟大蕭條的敘述何者不正確？
   (A) **經濟衰敗，每件事都令人沮喪不已。**
   (B) 許多人失去工作和家園。
   (C) 始於紐約股市崩盤的時候。
   (D) 羅斯福總統在這段期間內試圖使經濟好轉。

5. 經濟大蕭條期間，聯邦作家計畫試圖
   _____。
   (A) **使人們認識自己的城市並瞭解彼此**
   (B) 雇用作家來製作旅遊導覽
   (C) 製作關於國家經濟問題的書籍
   (D) 記錄人們生活多麼困苦

Try it!
1. walks of life
2. crash
3. project
4. unity
5. interviewed

---

a walk of life　行業	stock market　股市	guide　n.　指南
crash　n.　(股價) 暴跌	decline　n.　衰退	ethnic　adj.　種族的
project　n.　計畫	depression　n.　蕭條	former　adj.　之前的
unity　n.　團結	establish　v.　建立	slave　n.　奴隸
interview　v.　訪問	author　n.　作者	spirit　n.　精神

29 不只是紙鈔上的肖像
More Than an Image on a Bill

美國有許多著名發明家。不過，班傑明・富蘭克林也許是其中最有名的一位。雖然他同時也是位作家及哲學家，但富蘭克林最為世人所記得的，還是他的多項發明。

富蘭克林發明許多實用物品，原因通常是因為他需要它們。例如，富蘭克林戴眼鏡，但隨著他年紀越來越大，就需要另一副適合閱讀的眼鏡。兩副眼鏡換來換去讓富蘭克林覺得很麻煩，他決定發明一副能讓他同時看清楚遠處和近處的眼鏡。這些眼鏡就是如今的雙焦點眼鏡。富蘭克林也發明出特別的鐵爐——富蘭克林爐。它讓人們能以更安全的方式暖和屋子，所使用的木柴也比傳統壁爐少。

除此之外，你也許聽過富蘭克林著名的放風箏故事，但最先發現電力的人並非富蘭克林，他僅證明了閃電是電的一種形式。不過，從那次經驗中，富蘭克林獲得發明避雷針的知識，那是一種能使建築物和船隻避免遭到雷擊的裝置。

毫無疑問地，班傑明・富蘭克林發明許多有用物品。雖然他在政治上也有許多成就，寫了數本著名作品，他的肖像甚至被印在美國百元紙鈔上，但富蘭克林最為人知的，還是他的無數發明品。

1. 本篇文章主要是關於 _____ 。
　(A) 世界各地的著名發明家
　(B) 富蘭克林和他的發明品
　(C) 富蘭克林的作家生涯
　(D) 如何製作閱讀用的眼鏡

2. 根據文章內容，誰發現了電力？
　(A) 風箏。
　(B) 班傑明・富蘭克林。
　(C) 一名美國哲學家。
　(D) 我們無法由本文得知。

3. 富蘭克林發明東西通常是因為 _____ 。
　(A) 他希望能被世人懷念
　(B) 他想降低木柴的使用
　(C) 他需要那些東西
　(D) 他缺錢

4. 根據這篇文章，避雷針 _____ 。
　(A) 看起來像風箏
　(B) 協助人們安全地使屋子暖和
　(C) 能使建築物不受雷擊
　(D) 如今已不被使用

5. 下列何者也可作為本文標題？
　(A) 如何成為有名的發明家
　(B) 美國最有名的發明家
　(C) 班傑明・富蘭克林和他的眼鏡
　(D) 班傑明・富蘭克林發明品的重要

Try it!
1. image　　2. famous　　3. lightning
4. device　　5. inventor

image n. 肖像	philosopher n. 哲學家	without a doubt 無疑地
famous adj. 著名的	pair n. 一副；一雙	accomplish v. 達成
lightning n. 雷	bifocals n. 遠視近視兩用眼鏡	politics n. 政治
device n. 裝置	iron n. 鐵	bill n. 紙鈔
inventor n. 發明家	gain v. 獲得	remain v. 依然不變

30 希望
Hope

——愛蜜莉‧狄金森

希望有雙翅膀
棲息於靈魂之上
唱著沒有歌詞的曲調
從不停止

強風中聽聞最甜美的聲音
風暴襲來必定猛烈
它使溫暖眾多心靈的鳥兒
亦感到困窘

我曾在最寒冷的土地上
最陌生的海洋中聽見它的聲音
然而在絕境中
它從來沒有對我作出絲毫要求

1. 在詩的第一節，為何詩人說，希望從不止息地
   唱著曲調？
   (A) 因為希望不斷給予人面對問題的勇氣。
   (B) 因為希望能使人們唱歌時不走音。
   (C) 因為若人們心中有希望，歌就唱得好。
   (D) 因為從不停止歌唱的人將會成功。
2. 這名詩人將希望與 _____ 相比擬。
   (A) 羽毛　(B) 微風　(C) 風暴　**(D)** 鳥
3. 在詩的最後一節，最寒冷的土地與最陌生的
   海域，意指住起來很 _____ 的地方。
   (A) 寒冷　(B) 輕鬆　(C) 貧瘠　**(D)** 艱困
4. 最後兩行詩句使我們瞭解到，_____。
   (A) 艱困時期的報償就是希望
   (B) 希望從未要求任何回報
   (C) 希望是我們最不該放棄的東西

(D) 即使只剩微渺的希望，生活仍將繼續
5. 這首詩的整體調性是 _____。
   (A) 負面的　　　　　(B) 變動的
   (C) 軟弱的　　　　　**(D)** 鼓勵人心的

Try it!

1. chilly　　2. soul　　3. tune
4. feathers　5. ask...of

---

chilly　adj.　寒冷的
soul　n.　靈魂
tune　n.　曲調
feather　n.　羽毛

ask...of　請求
perch　v.　棲息
gale　n.　強風
sore　n.　劇烈的

storm　n.　暴風雨
abash　v.　使困窘
extremity　n.　絕境
crumb　n.　麵包屑

文字之外
Beyond Words

身為英語系學生，你可能已經曉得，照字面直譯並不是個翻譯的好方法。以「你好嗎？」(How's it going?) 這個句子為例，若你用字典查出每個單字的意思，然後把這些字照著你母語中的意思一個個直接放在一起，結果會如何？很可能你會得出一個毫無意義的句子。

通常，英文系學生首先被教導的就是要明白每個字的意思。然而，溝通從來就不只是把所有的字放在一起，你必須以正確的順序擺放它們，這時就需要文法規則。若說話者搞錯了字詞順序，人們就會很難瞭解彼此表達之意。字詞順序的改變，往往也會影響整句話的意思。例如，「她只讀《新聞週刊》」(She only reads *Newsweek*.) 這句話和「只有她讀《新聞週刊》」(Only she reads *Newsweek*.) 意思不太一樣。不過，有時字詞順序的改變並不會影響整句話的意思。舉例來說：「韋恩把食物給了乞丐」(Wayne gave food to the beggar.) 跟「韋恩給了乞丐食物」(Wayne gave the beggar food.) 的意思是一樣的。

因此，進階學習者必須超越字詞學習這個層次。隨著閱讀量增大，能快速分辨出哪些字適合連用、哪些字不適合。一旦你掌握箇中訣竅，聽起來就會很像以英語為母語的人了。

1. 本篇文章主要是關於 _____。
   (**A**) 如何精通英語
   (B) 如何改變字詞順序
   (C) 如何將英語翻譯為中文
   (D) 為何需要學習文法規則

2. 翻譯英語句子最好的方法是 _____。
   (A) 照字面直譯
   (B) 查出每個單字的意思
   (C) 改變字詞順序
   (**D**) 以上皆非。

3. 若你搞錯句子中的字詞順序，_____。
   (A) 此時就需要文法規則
   (**B**) 別人會很難瞭解你想表達的意思
   (C) 句子的意思仍然不變
   (D) 人們將能很快分辨出哪些字適合連用

4. 第一段中的「tongue」意指 _____。
   (**A**) 一種語言
   (B) 某種特定說話方式
   (C) 某種又長又細的東西
   (D) 位於嘴巴中的柔軟部位
   → tongue 可以表「口才」、「舌狀物」、「舌頭」，於此表示「語言」。

5. 下列敘述何者正確？
   (A) 溝通就是把所有的字放在一起。
   (B) 英語系學生往往會照字面意思直譯。
   (**C**) 「將某物給某人」(give something to someone) 和「給某人某物」(give someone something) 意思相同。
   (D) 若改變字詞順序，人們依然可以瞭解彼此欲表達之意。

Try it!

1. nonsense
2. came into play
3. translating
4. look up
5. working on

---

nonsense n. 胡說	work on 著手進行	rule n. 規則
come into play 造成影響	tongue n. 語言	beggar n. 乞丐
translate v. 翻譯	typically adv. 通常	advanced adj. 進階的
look up 查找	order n. 順序	native adj. 本地出生的

32 風暴命名有學問
What's in a Name of a Storm?

熱帶氣旋是一種風暴，形成於世界上最熱之處，亦即熱帶。這種風暴繞著圈快速地移動，可帶來時速高達 60 公里以上的強風。在世界各地，這種風暴有不同名稱。它在亞太地區被稱為「颱風」，在美洲則被稱為「颶風」，2005 年侵襲美國東南部著名的卡崔娜颶風即為一例。

世界氣象組織密切觀察熱帶氣旋，並發出預報和警告，該組織也以 A 到 Z 的順序列出風暴之名。若某年第一個風暴的名字是艾爾 (Al)，下一個風暴即可能被命名為芭芭拉 (Barbara)。這份名單上沒有以 O、U、X、Y 和 Z 為開頭的名字，因為很少名字以這些字母為首。

因此，當一個氣旋在海上形成時，科學家會從名單中挑選出一個名字，男性或女性的名字都有可能。然而，在亞洲地區的國家，名單內容稍有不同。使用動物和植物的名字比用人名來得普遍，這些名字讓大眾更容易記得對風暴所發佈的最新消息。

1. 本篇文章主要是關於 _____ 。
   (A) 亞太地區的氣旋
   (B) 熱帶氣旋的名字
   (C) 熱帶氣旋的破壞性
   (D) 颱風和颶風的不同
   → 選項 A、C、D 太狹隘。
2. 熱帶氣旋的命名清單是依照 _____ 順序排列。
   (A) 時間　(B) 數字　**(C) 拼字**　(D) 重要性
3. 熱帶氣旋的名字可以是 _____ 。
   (A) 男性名字　　　(B) 女性名字

(C) 動物名字　　　**(D) 以上皆是。**
4. 以下何者可能為風暴的名字？
   (A) 奧立佛 (Oliver)。　(B) 約克 (York)。
   (C) 柔伊 (Zoe)。　　**(D) 溫蒂 (Wendy)。**
5. 下列敘述何者正確？
   (A) 熱帶是世界上最熱的地區。
   (B) 在亞太地區，熱帶氣旋被稱為颶風。
   (C) 熱帶氣旋形成於世界上最冷的地方。
   (D) 在美洲，氣旋通常以植物和動物的名字命名。

🍦 Try it!
1. forecast　　2. struck　　3. organization
4. warning　　5. catch up with

---

forecast　n.　預報
strike　v.　侵襲
organization　n.　機構
warning　n.　警告

catch up with　趕上
tropical　adj.　熱帶的
cyclone　n.　氣旋
circle　n.　圓圈

typhoon　n.　颱風
hurricane　n.　颶風
meteorological　adj.　氣象的
latest　adj.　最新的

33 企鵝危機
Penguins in Danger

自然界中最受喜愛的鳥類之一——企鵝——很可能會絕種。事實上，在不久的將來，總共 17 種企鵝其中的 10 種可能完全消失，在過去十年左右，企鵝數量銳減了百分之三十。在進一步探討這項危機的原因之前，以下是這種鳥類的一些資料。

企鵝是黑白分明的鳥類，以南半球地區為家，如南極、紐西蘭和澳洲。牠們生活在冷水域，以魚和蝦類為食。企鵝不會飛，但卻是游泳健將。

讓我們回到造成危機的原因。首先，全球暖化帶來了企鵝的災難。因為企鵝賴以維生的海中生物無法在暖水中生存，企鵝很可能因為缺乏食物而餓死。另一方面，石油探勘以及漏油則危害到企鵝的生命。最後，海獅或海豹總是在獵食企鵝。

雖然對企鵝已造成的傷害無法復原，但令人安慰的是，有許多人試圖幫助牠們。幾年前，一場漏油事件使南非百分之四十的企鵝全身覆滿油污，有數千名人類樂於伸出援手清理這些鳥類，他們照顧這些鳥類直到牠們恢復健康，再將牠們放回大自然中。

1. 這篇文章主要談論的是 _____ 。
   (A) 為何許多人喜歡企鵝
   (B) 如何拯救企鵝免於絕種
   (C) 為何企鵝面臨絕種危機
   (D) 為何企鵝是游泳健將
   → 選項 A、B、D 均沒被提及或說明。

2. 在不久的將來，多少種企鵝會滅絕？
   (A) 10。 (B) 17。 (C) 30。 (D) 40。

3. 第一段中「shrink」意指 _____ 。
   (A) 在數量上變多
   (B) 在數量上變少
   (C) 退開或閃開某物
   (D) 以熱水洗滌時變得更小
   → shrink 可以表示「縮水」、「畏縮」，於此表示「變少」。

4. 什麼會導致企鵝絕種？
   (A) 石油漏油。 (B) 鑽探石油。
   (C) 全球暖化。 **(D) 以上皆是。**

5. 下列敘述何者正確？
   (A) 世界上總共有 17 種企鵝。
   (B) 企鵝是白黑分明的海洋生物。
   (C) 企鵝以北半球地區為家。
   (D) 由於全球暖化，企鵝可能因為缺水而絕種。

🌱 Try it!

1. crisis   2. survived   3. die out
4. end up   5. shrank

---

crisis n. 危機	penguin n. 企鵝	spell v. 意味著
survive v. 生還	species n. 物種	drill v. 鑽 (孔)
die out 絕種	decade n. 十年	leak n. 洩漏
end up 最後…	feed on 以…為食	undo v. 復原
shrink v. 縮減	global warming 地球暖化	spill n. 溢出

34 國際狗狗節
International Dog Day

每年的 8 月 26 日是國際狗狗節。這是一個特別的日子，用來慶祝和感謝狗狗帶給我們的快樂和愛。在這一天，人們會做各式各樣的事情來表達對狗狗的愛。以下是一些例子。

領養狗	如果你正在考慮養狗，這天可能是個好日子。許多收容所裡的狗狗都需要家，收養狗可以為你和狗都帶來歡樂。
花時間陪伴你的狗	帶你的狗去散步、到公園玩耍，或單純只是依偎在沙發上。狗狗喜歡受到關注，花時間在一起可以讓你們的聯結更強烈。
給予零食	為你的狗狗做一頓特別的餐點或準備零食。你也可以給牠們新玩具或舒適的床。狗狗會很喜歡這些小事，這讓牠們感到被愛。
在收容所幫忙	如果你沒有養狗，可以花時間到動物收容所當志工。你可以透過餵食、梳理毛髮或陪伴玩耍來協助照顧牠們的工作。
捐款給狗狗慈善機構	支持致力於保護狗狗安全和快樂的團體。你可以捐錢、食物、玩具或其他東西。每份付出都有助於改善狗狗的生活。

狗被認為是我們最好的朋友，因為牠們忠誠且充滿愛心。人們把狗當作朋友，已經有很長一段時間了，而狗也在狩獵和守衛這些事情上幫助我們。如今，許多人都養狗當寵物，並把牠們當家人一樣對待。狗狗每天都給我們愛，國際狗狗節正是一個回饋一點愛的機會！

1. 國際狗狗節的主要目的為何？
   (A) 販賣特別的狗零食。
   (B) 讚揚狗狗並表達對牠們的感謝。
   (C) 推廣狗狗的領養。
   (D) 舉辦狗展。

2. 根據本文，慶祝國際狗狗節建議用什麼方式來進行？
   (A) 買一隻新狗。
   (B) 參加狗展。
   (C) 只捐款給狗狗慈善機構。
   (D) 花時間陪伴自己的狗。

3. 文中提到的「bond」是什麼意思？
   (A) 財務投資。　　**(B) 關聯或關係。**
   (C) 一個狗的品種。　(D) 一種狗吃的零食。

4. 根據本文，為什麼有些人把狗看作他們最好的朋友？
   (A) 因為狗擅長狩獵。
   (B) 因為狗很會保護人。
   (C) 因為狗既忠誠又充滿愛心。
   (D) 因為狗很容易訓練。

5. 作者在最後一段提到「give some love back」，是要表示什麼？
   (A) 回報狗狗帶來的愛與陪伴。
   (B) 對陌生人付出部分愛心。
   (C) 用愛心交換物質財產。
   (D) 把愛保留到未來使用。

Try it!
1. adopt　　2. shelter　　3. volunteered
4. cuddle　　5. happiness

---

adopt v. 收養，領養	shelter n. 收容所	attention n. 關注，注意
happiness n. 幸福；快樂	volunteer v. 擔任志工	appreciate v. 感激；欣賞
cuddle v. 依偎，擁抱	groom v. 理毛，梳毛	charity n. 慈善機構

35 看進未來
Looking Into the Future

一天，伽利略接到一位荷蘭朋友的來信。信上寫著，「這裡有個名叫立普樹的人，他製作了一種非常奇妙的眼鏡。我跟他約了碰面，要他給我看那種眼鏡。當時，遠處似乎有一位美麗的女士。我透過那種眼鏡看她，在那一瞬間，我真的覺得她就站在我面前，實在太不可思議了！我以為她在我伸手可及之處，所以我伸出手去碰她，結果卻跌倒了。立普樹扶我起來，大笑不已，因為那名女士其實離我們非常遠。」

這封信給伽利略帶來一些靈感。他決定自己來製作這種鏡片，甚至是一種更好的鏡片。「有了這種鏡片，」伽利略心想，「我不只能看見遠處的女士，甚至能看見月亮！」他很快開始製作自己的鏡片。他把它命名為「望遠鏡」(在希臘文中，「tele」意指「遠」，而「scope」意指「看」。) 當伽利略終於完成時，他用這種鏡片觀察夜空。他幾乎說不出話來，月亮幾乎就像在他面前一樣。立普樹能看見遠方，但伽利略卻能看見天空的另一端。

1. 本篇文章主要是關於 _____ 。
   (A) 伽利略的一生
   (B) 望遠鏡的發明
   (C) 伽利略的朋友寫給他的信
   (D) 「望遠鏡」這個字的起源
2. 伽利略很可能是個 _____ 。
   (A) 作家　　　　　(B) 醫生
   (C) 老師　　　　　**(D) 天文學家**
   → 從他想觀月可推知，他是個天文學家 astronomer。

3. 伽利略的朋友為何會跌倒？
   (A) 因為他笑個不停。
   (B) 因為立普樹把他絆倒。
   (C) 因為有一名女子站在他面前。
   (D) 因為他試圖用手去碰一名其實位於遠處的女子。
4. 出現在第一段的片語「get to one's feet」意指 _____ 。
   (A) 站起來
   (B) 穿鞋子
   (C) 四處走
   (D) 非常努力地去做某事
   → get to one's feet 表示「站起來」。
5. 下列敘述何者正確？
   (A) 伽利略的朋友是名希臘人。
   (B) 在希臘文中，「scope」的意思是「看」。
   (C) 一個名叫立普樹的男子寫信給伽利略。
   (D) 伽利略的朋友作出一種非常奇妙的眼鏡。

Try it!
1. fell over　　2. actually　　3. reached for
4. of my own　5. unbelievable

fall over　跌倒	of one's own　自己的	instant　n.　片刻
actually　adv.　事實上	unbelievable　adj.　難以置信的	get to one's feet　站起來
reach for　伸手觸 (或拿)	far away　遙遠的	telescope　n.　望遠鏡

36 福袋
Fukubukuro Lucky Bags

在日本，有種特殊的東西叫做「福袋」，又稱為「幸運袋」。這些袋子裝滿了驚喜商品，並在某些時段以大幅折扣出售。每個福袋都有特定的主題，例如美容產品或電腦配件。日本人喜歡這些福袋，因為它們提供了一種趣味的方式來試試運氣，看能不能買得物超所值。

儘管沒有人確知是誰最先在日本銷售第一批福袋，但關於它的起源有一些有趣的說法。有人說它始於江戶時代一家名為越後屋的和服店，也就是後來的三越百貨。為了處理掉多餘的庫存，他們在袋子裡裝滿了未使用的布料，並於冬季特賣時以打折出售。這種做法變得非常流行，而這個傳統也一直延續到今日。

另一個說法和大丸屋有關，也就是後來我們所知道的大丸百貨。他們想出了在節慶和新年期間販售福袋的想法。這讓福袋的傳統在日本各地流傳開來。另外，也有一些說法宣稱福袋始於之後的明治時代。然而，無論何時開始，所有說法都一致認為，這項傳統源自一家販賣和服布料的店家。

在日本的新年期間，你可以在貨架上找到福袋。有些商家會在 12 月 29 日就提早開賣。也有些知名商家甚至會要求你提前幾個月預訂福袋！

如果你錯過了新年特賣，不用擔心。一年中的其他時間，也都還是能找到福袋大特賣。當你造訪日本時，多留意福袋的標誌，然後好好享受驚喜吧！

1. 這篇文章的主要目的為何？
 (A) 批評日本傳統的商業化現象。
 (B) 告知讀者百貨公司的歷史。
 (C) 描述和服布料在現代日本的受歡迎程度。
 (D) 介紹並解說福袋的傳統。

2. 根據本文，日本有些商家何時開始販賣福袋？
 (A) 2 月 14 日。　　(B) 7 月 1 日。
 (C) 12 月 29 日。　　(D) 10 月 31 日。

3. 關於福袋的傳統，下列何者可從本文推論得知？
 (A) 它是由造訪日本的觀光客發明的。
 (B) 它是從一間電腦用品店開始的。
 (C) 它只發生在新年特賣期間。
 (D) 它提供了一種取得特價商品的趣味方式。

4. 這篇文章最可能出現在哪裡？
 (A) 介紹日本的旅遊指南。
 (B) 日本史的教科書。
 (C) 電腦科學主題的雜誌。
 (D) 百貨公司的廣告。

5. 作者對福袋的態度為何？
 (A) 批判。　　　　(B) 中立。
 (C) 感到興奮。　　(D) 漠不關心。

 Try it!

1. discount　　2. reserve　　3. stock
4. sign　　　5. purchase

---

discount　n.　折扣　　　　sign　n.　標誌　　　　festival　n.　節慶
reserve　v.　預約，預定　　purchase　v.　購買　　claim　v.　宣稱
stock　n.　存貨，庫存　　　theme　n.　主題　　　fabric　n.　布料

37 好成績的代價？
Straight A's at the Cost of Sleep?

在求學時期，幾乎每個人在課堂上都有過這種經驗：打呵欠。你感到眼皮沈重，上半身前後搖晃。你的書掉到地上，發出足以驚醒同學的一聲「砰！」。

研究顯示，一名學生每天至少需要八小時睡眠，但大部分學生都睡眠不足。有些父母樂見孩子們熬夜，因為得到好成績最重要，所以讀書讀晚一點是值得的。因此在台灣，很多學生早上六點起床，晚上六點離開學校，十點才從補習班回到家，而回家後還有一堆功課要做！他們幾乎沒有一夜好眠。有些父母為此感到困擾，當他們看到孩子無法在課堂上專心或筋疲力盡地回到家，心裡感到很難受。

功課太多是許多學生共同的抱怨，他們表示必須花許多時間才能趕上進度或超越別人。也有許多學生不知道該如何以更有效率的方式把事情做完。許多專家建議學生養成良好學習習慣，例如「當下就開始」、「課堂上要專心」，或組成讀書會來協助彼此。他們都希望學生們能睡得飽，同時課業表現好。

1. 本篇文章主要在協助學生 _____。
  (A) 認真上課　　　(B) 組成學習小組
  (C) 養成良好睡眠習慣 (**D**) **睡得飽表現也好**
2. 第一段在描述學生課堂上 _____ 的情形。
  (**A**) **打瞌睡**　　　　(B) 醒來
  (C) 跟上進度　　　(D) 超越別人
  → doze off 表示「打瞌睡」，catch up 表示「趕上」，get ahead 表示「領先」。

3. 許多學生抱怨 _____。
  (A) 成績很差　　　(B) 要在早上六點起床
  (C) 睡不飽　　　(**D**) **功課太多**
4. 第二段片語「burn the midnight oil」意指 _____。
  (A) 在課堂上打瞌睡
  (**B**) **讀書或工作到深夜**
  (C) 承擔某事後果
  (D) 試圖做太多件事而變得非常疲累
  → burn the midnight oil 表示「熬夜讀書或工作」。
5. 下列敘述何者正確？
  (A) 許多專家建議學生養成良好睡眠習慣。
  (B) 研究顯示，大多數學生每天都至少能睡八小時。
  (C) 專家們都希望，學生能睡得更多並比現在更努力讀書。
  (**D**) **有些父母樂於看到孩子們熬夜讀書，但有些父母正好相反。**

Try it!
1. worth　　2. to and fro　3. efficient
4. at least　　5. concentrate

worth　adj.　值得的	yawn　v.　打呵欠	cram school　補習班
to and fro　來回地	eyelid　n.　眼皮	barely　adv.　幾乎沒有
efficient　adj.　有效率的	rock　v.　搖晃	focus　v.　專心
at least　至少	drop　v.　掉落	suggest　v.　建議
concentrate　v.　專心	bang　n.　砰的一聲	habit　n.　習慣

38 省到就是賺到
A Dollar Saved Is a Dollar Earned

　　當人們需要更多錢時，大部分會額外加班或去找更高薪的工作。然而，賺更多錢並非增加銀行存款的唯一方式。其實，只要聰明地用錢，你就能不換工作或額外加班而達到這項目的。

　　省錢的一個重要步驟就是定出預算。你應該留意賺了多少錢，以及把錢花到哪裡去了。一個實用的方法就是隨身帶著小筆記本，把每筆花費記錄下來，只要仔細檢視筆記，你就能找出省錢之道。例如，愛喝咖啡的人可能會發現自己花太多錢在咖啡店買咖啡，因此，就可以改成自己在家泡咖啡來省錢。使用折價券也是另一種省錢之道。許多購物者發現，使用折價券能讓他們的雜貨開支減少百分之五十。

　　總體來說，創意思考是省錢的關鍵。除了以上所提到的幾個想法之外，有些學生使用免費的網路電話服務如 LINE 來減少電話費。透過聰明地用錢，你可能會驚訝的發現，自己擁有比實際所需還多的錢。正如那句名言所說，「省一塊錢，就等於賺了一塊錢。」

1. 根據這篇文章，作者認為 _____ 。
   (A) 最好的省錢之道就是換工作
   (B) 使用折價券無助於省錢
   (C) 人們完全不應該購物
   (D) 創意思考對省錢來說很重要
2. 下列何者不是省錢的方式？
   (A) 購物時使用折價券。
   (B) 購買最新型的手機。
   (C) 在大拍賣時購物。
   (D) 在家裡自己泡咖啡喝，而不是去咖啡店買。

3. 定出預算有助於省錢，因為我們能 _____ 。
   (A) 知道每個月賺了多少錢
   (B) 更意識到花了多少錢
   (C) 知道哪裡可取得折價券
   (D) 學習如何在家裡泡咖啡
4. 下列敘述何者正確？
   (A) 兼差是賺更多錢的唯一方法。
   (B) 定出預算有助於善加管理金錢。
   (C) 為了省錢，有些人一年才買一次衣服。
   (D) 換工作有助人們減少支出或費用。
5. 有些人使用 LINE 來減少 _____ 。
   (A) 雜貨費用　　　　(B) 咖啡支出
   (C) 服飾開銷　　　　(D) 電話費

 Try it!
1. Instead　　2. coupon　　3. overtime
4. budget　　5. review

instead　adv.　取而代之	earn　v.　賺取	extra　adj.　額外的
coupon　n.　折價券	increase　v.　增加	step　n.　步驟
overtime　n.　加班	account　n.　帳戶	practical　adj.　實用的
budget　n.　預算	achieve　v.　達成	grocery　adj.　雜貨的
review　v.　檢查	goal　n.　目標	mention　v.　提及

39 芳香療法：不只聞聞而已
Aromatherapy: Not Only for the Nose

你是否曾想過，你聞到的味道能影響你的感覺？一種名為「芳香療法」的新治療方式聲稱，味道能影響我們的感覺，甚至健康。

1920 年代，一名法國科學家首創「芳香療法」這個字。它結合了「芳香」（味道），和「療法」（治療）。基本上，芳香療法使用精油以及從植物萃取出的化合物。進行芳香療法時，精油的味道會被吸入，換句話說，一個人要拿著裝精油的瓶子靠近鼻子，然後深深吸氣。此外，精油也可以直接按摩在皮膚上或滴入熱水澡盆中。

芳香療法非常受到想紓解壓力者的歡迎。更有甚者，如今有些醫生在醫院使用芳香療法來減輕病患疼痛，特別是承受嚴重分娩陣痛的孕婦。

但有些人對芳香療法發出批評。他們認為沒有科學證據顯示這種療法真的有效。此外，有些芳香療法產品聞起來很不錯，實際上卻是假造的。

即使有這些批評聲浪，芳香療法的魅力不減反增，但對於它是否有用的爭辯也仍在持續。許多人對芳香療法仍抱持懷疑態度，不知到底是有效的療法或只是賺錢工具，只有留待時間來證明一切。

1.「芳香療法」這個字意指 _____ 。
  (A) 醫院中特別的熱水泡澡法
  (B) 一種吸進蒸氣的方式
  (C) 一種使用油的傳統按摩
  (D) 一種使用精油的治療法

2. 哪種材料用在芳香療法中？
  (A) 藥物。
  (B) 從海水萃取出的化合物。
  (C) 水。
  (D) 精油。

3. 下列何者不是使用精油的正確方式？
  (A) 將它們吸入。
  (B) 將它們按摩滲透到皮膚裡。
  (C) 將它們加入飲用水中。
  (D) 將它們滴入泡澡盆中。

4. 根據這篇文章，誰特別需要芳香療法？
  (A) 一直哭的小男孩。
  (B) 即將臨盆的女子。
  (C) 傷到手指的工人。
  (D) 體重過重的青少年。

5. 下列敘述何者不正確？
  (A) 人類的感覺可能會受到味道影響。
  (B) 芳香療法已被證明非常有效。
  (C) 關於芳香療法是否有效的爭論仍然持續中。
  (D) 有些聞起來不錯的芳香療法產品可能是假貨。

Try it!
1. influencing 2. criticized 3. relief
4. Combine 5. breathing

influence v. 影響	aroma n. 芳香	extract v. 萃取
criticize v. 批評	therapy n. 療法	basically adv. 基本上
relief n. (痛苦) 減輕	treatment n. 治療	massage v. 按摩
combine v. 結合	essential oil 精油	labor n. 分娩
breathe v. 呼吸	compound n. 化合物	fake adj. 假的

40 就是要健康
All About Healthy Living

由於長時間坐在桌子前及不良飲食習慣的趨勢，如今人們有了更粗的腰圍及更多成年疾病。以下是一些保持健康的小秘訣。

1. 吃得健康：飲食內容最好由全穀類、蔬菜和水果組成。吃含有高纖維和低「壞」脂肪的食物會使你健康。關鍵在於每樣食物都均衡攝取，並且長期持續這樣的飲食習慣。

2. 多動動身體：試著每天至少運動 30 分鐘。例如快走，若能規律進行，不只能幫你維持身材，更能降低壓力並改善睡眠和記憶。

然而，完美的健康狀態更是身體與心靈雙方面的平衡。以下是兩個改善心理健康的小秘訣。

1. 有支持自己的團體：跟自己生命中重要的人保持密切關係。你的家人和好友能幫你度過生命中的許多起伏。他們往往能照顧你的情感需求，協助你從不同角度看事情並更清楚地思考。

2. 正向思考：正向思考已被證實能在人類心中產生更強的希望感，驅使人們朝目標努力，並更快樂地生活。

1. 這篇文章主要是關於 _____ 。
　(A) 如何吃得健康　　(B) 如何減重
　(C) 如何保持健康　(D) 如何處理壓力
　→ 選項 A、B、D 太狹隘。
2. _____ 可能導致疾病。
　(A) 不良飲食習慣　　(B) 長時間坐著
　(C) 腰圍變粗　　　　**(D) 以上皆是。**

3. 每天運動無法幫助人們 _____ 。
　(A) 保持健康　　　　(B) 釋放壓力
　(C) 睡得好　　　　　**(D) 增加腰圍**
4. 第五段中的片語 「ups and downs」 意指 _____ 。
　(A) 一個人的義務或責任
　(B) 往上和下移動
　(C) 好壞交雜
　(D) 方向的改變
　→ ups and downs 表示「人生起起伏伏」。
5. _____ 有助於人們保持心理和身體的健康。
　(A) 規律的運動
　(B) 正向思考
　(C) 來自家人和朋友的愛與關懷
　(D) 以上皆是。

> 💡 **Try it!**
> 1. stick to　　2. improved　　3. Thanks to
> 4. ups and downs　　5. stress

---

stick to　堅持
improve　v.　改進
thanks to　由於
ups and downs　人生起伏
stress　n.　壓力；緊張

tendency　n.　趨勢
waistline　n.　腰圍
disease　n.　疾病
fit　adj.　健康的
grain　n.　穀物

brisk　adj.　迅速的
emotional　adj.　情緒的
support　n.　支持
angle　n.　角度
positively　adv.　積極地

世界水資源協會：拯救水資源
World Water Council: To the Rescue of Water

　　世界水資源協會是一個由來自世界各地的成員所組成的組織。其目的在於討論保存、保護及管理世界各地淡水資源的更佳方式。會員們努力將這些技術教導給世界各地正作出與水資源問題有關之重大決議的政府、大公司和其他重要人士。

　　在許多解決政府之間水資源問題的國際會議成功舉辦後，一個特別委員會於 1995 年成立，以決定世界水資源協會的目標為何。世界水資源協會於是在 1996 年六月正式成立，主要總部設在法國馬賽市。

　　世界水資源協會的主要活動大多在於舉辦特別會議，使全球的重要人士和專家齊聚一堂。世界水資源協會亦努力確保全世界的人都能使用淡水，並致力將水運送到貧窮國家。該協會組成了許多團體，例如水資源合作設施，並運用來自會員的錢來協助減少世界各地的水資源問題。

　　對世界上的人而言，保存及保護淡水資源是非常重要的。大多數政府已認知到這項需要，並積極協助世界水資源協會的計畫成功執行。

1. 本篇文章主要是關於＿＿＿＿＿＿。
   (A) 保存水資源的重要
   (B) 作出重大決定的過程
   (C) 世界水資源協會的介紹
   (D) 馬賽市的歷史
2. 世界水資源協會何時正式成立？
   (A) 1977 年。　　　　(B) 1995 年。
   (C) 1996 年。　　　　(D) 1997 年。

3. 第三段中的「it」意指＿＿＿＿＿＿。
   (A) 貧窮國家　　　　(B) 大公司
   (C) 法國政府　　　　(D) 世界水資源協會
4. 下列關於世界水資源協會的敘述何者正確？
   (A) 它討論保護水資源的更佳方式。
   (B) 它教導大公司如何生產飲用水。
   (C) 它致力於將水運到許多已開發國家。
   (D) 它賺取會員的錢。
5. 我們能從本文得知＿＿＿＿＿＿。
   (A) 大多數政府支持世界水資源協會正在進行的事務
   (B) 許多公司並不想協助世界水資源協會
   (C) 人們不想學習與水資源問題有關的技術
   (D) 如今沒有其他團體協助解決水資源問題

Try it!
1. recognize　　2. conserve　　3. available
4. purpose　　5. manage

recognize　v.　承認
conserve　v.　保護 (自然資源)
available　adj.　可獲得的
purpose　n.　目的
manage　v.　處理

discuss　v.　討論
protect　v.　保護
technique　n.　技巧
solve　v.　解決
committee　n.　委員會

headquarters　n.　總部
set up　設立
worldwide　adj.　全世界的
facility　n.　設施
actively　adv.　主動地

42 給予之道
The Gift of Giving

　　當我為週六的車庫拍賣會準備拍賣品時，一張照片吸引了我的目光。那是我和我同學們在八歲時的合照。它顯示當時我們每個人所穿衣服的尺寸，而這張照片深深觸動我的內心。於是我叫兩個孩子連恩和潔西卡過來看這張照片，並告訴他們，「看，有好多人窮困得連合適的衣服都沒得穿。這個週末就讓大家看看，我們可以作出多大貢獻。我們每個人都來免費送出幾樣東西，怎麼樣？」

　　我告訴孩子們，他們可以從自己已經不用的舊東西開始著手。連恩找出好幾箱他長大已經用不著的舊玩具兵和穿不下的 T 恤。我對連恩微笑，然後轉頭看潔西卡拿出什麼來。結果我看見她拿出自己最喜歡的洋娃娃，蓋兒，還很新而且被照顧得很好。我說，「潔西，妳不用這麼做的！妳那麼喜歡這個洋娃娃。」潔西卡回答道，「媽咪，如果蓋兒能讓我快樂，也能讓其他女孩子快樂。再見了，蓋兒。」她邊說邊揮手與洋娃娃道別。

　　我相當震撼。潔西卡的舉動讓我深思不已。給別人自己不要的東西很容易，但分享自己的最愛卻不容易。設身處地為他人著想，並給予他人最需要的東西，我想，就是愛吧。

1. 本篇文章主要是關於 _____ 。
　(A) 適合在車庫拍賣會拍賣的物品
　(B) 非常貧窮的人們
　(C) 無私地去愛和幫助他人
　(D) 把某人不要的東西給別人
2. 文章敘述者建議在車庫拍賣會中怎麼做？

　(A) 清理車庫。
　(B) 賺一些錢。
　(C) 一起看照片。
　(D) 免費把一些東西送人。
3. 潔西卡想送給別人的東西是什麼？
　(A) 舊 T 恤。　　　　(B) 舊玩具兵。
　(C) 她最愛的洋娃娃。 (D) 一個舊車庫。
4. 片語「put yourself in one's shoes」意指
　_____ 。
　(A) 穿上別人的鞋子
　(B) 為了某人原因做某些事情
　(C) 做原本由某人做的工作
　(D) 想像自己身在另一個人的處境中
5. 下列敘述何者正確？
　(A) 潔西卡要送給別人的洋娃娃又舊又破。
　(B) 把不想要的東西送給別人一點也不容易。
　(C) 文章敘述者建議她的孩子把自己喜愛的東西送給別人。
　(D) 潔西卡將自己的洋娃娃送給別人，希望它能帶給其他女孩子快樂。
　→ put yourself in one's shoes 表示「設身處地為他人著想」。

> ### Try it!
> 1. stuff　　　　　2. give away
> 3. grown out of　4. caught my eye
> 5. anymore

---

stuff　n.　物品　　　　catch one's eye　吸引某人目光　　for free　免費的
give away　捐贈　　　　anymore　adv.　(不) 再　　　　wave　v.　揮手
grow out of　長大而穿不下　garage sale　舊物拍賣　　　impressed　adj.　印象深刻的

43 銀髮經濟
Silver Economy

我們的世界正在發生變化，越來越多的人正在變老。這為全球經濟創造了新的機會，即所謂的「銀髮經濟」。這種特別的經濟專注於為老年人 (即 50 歲或以上的老年人) 生產商品和服務。

銀髮經濟的重要元素之一是旅遊業。許多退休人員經常旅行。他們拜訪新的地方、乘坐遊輪、住酒店。一些公司為老年旅行者規劃特殊的假期，例如為 50 歲以上的人提供旅行。此外，一些飯店和餐廳專門為老年人服務，因為他們了解老年人的需求。

另一個重要生意是醫療保健。老年人經常需要醫療預約的幫助，例如去看牙醫或去醫院。有些老人住在養老院，那裡有專業人員整天照顧他們。在一些國家，甚至專門為老年人設立了醫院來滿足他們的需求。

還有許多企業出售針對老年人的產品。一些公司生產易於穿脫的特殊服裝。其他公司則生產帶有大按鈕和簡單功能選單的特殊手機，比普通手機更容易使用。有些汽車為年長的駕駛者設計了更大的座椅和照後鏡。甚至還有更容易駕駛和停車的汽車。

未來，銀髮經濟將更加重要。到 2050 年，全球 65 歲以上人口將達到約 20 億。這佔四分之一的人口。因此，企業應該要開始關注年長的客戶，因為他們提供最棒的商機。

1. 這篇文章主要是關於什麼內容？
　(A) 專注於生產珍貴金屬的經濟。
　(B) 關心婦女的經濟。
　(C) 支持所有工人的經濟。
　(D) 為老年人生產商品的經濟。

2. 下列哪一項描述了本文中提到的生意順序？
　(A) 特殊產品 → 旅遊 → 醫療保健。
　(B) 特殊產品 → 醫療保健 → 旅遊。
　(C) 旅遊 → 醫療保健 → 特殊產品。
　(D) 醫療保健 → 旅遊 → 特殊產品。

3. 下列何者是為老年人設計的產品例子？
　(A) 時尚的衣服。
　(B) 具有高科技功能的電話。
　(C) 配備強力引擎的汽車。
　(D) 具有易於使用功能的汽車。

4. 下列哪一項是銀髮經濟的面向？
　(A) 銷售兒童玩具。
　(B) 為退休人員提供旅遊套裝行程。
　(C) 為青少年生產高科技產品。
　(D) 為年輕人創造時尚潮流。

5. 下列哪一張是養老院的照片？
　(A) 家庭。　　　　　**(B) 養老院。**
　(C) 托嬰中心。　　　(D) 寵物訓練學校。

🎨 **Try it!**

1. cruise　　　2. Medical　　　3. elderly
4. global　　　5. Tourism

---

global　adj.　全球的
tourism　n.　旅遊業
cruise　n.　郵輪

elderly　adj.　年邁的
medical　adj.　醫療的
economy　n.　經濟

retired　adj.　退休的
appointment　n.　預約
professional　n.　專業人員

44 真正博學多才的人：李奧納多・達文西
A Real Renaissance Man: Leonardo da Vinci

　　義大利人李奧納多・達文西出生在文藝復興時期，那是歐洲十四世紀到十七世紀期間，一段意味著「重生」的時代。在那段時間裡，科學和藝術領域有許多美好的新開始和新創意出現。博學之士想要瞭解世界、促進社會發展，並作出許多壯舉。達文西是個真正博學多聞之人：他是名優越的數學家、音樂家、畫家以及發明家。達文西用他偉大的天賦，展現人類如何有力地思考和行動。他不只是當代人的代表，更是放眼未來的人。

　　達文西畫出許多機器和工具的草圖，雖然大多數從未成為實際器具，他的概念卻啟發了後來的發明家。事實上，他的許多原創概念在他死後幾百年都成真了。

　　達文西是第一個策劃現代坦克車這種機器的人，他也發明了一艘能在海面下移動的船。達文西對於能讓人飛起來的機器也很有興趣。據說，他對直昇機的發想激勵了伊格・塞考斯基這位日後的直昇機製作大師。達文西想讓人類上達天空，而他真的策動人們展翅飛翔。

1. 達文西並不是一個＿＿＿＿＿。
　(A) 數學家 (B) 音樂家 (C) 畫家 **(D) 政治家**
2. 本篇文章的主題在於＿＿＿＿＿。
　(A) 伊格・塞考斯基的一生
　(B) 文藝復興時期人類的發明品
　(C) 李奧納多・達文西的重要性
　(D) 李奧納多・達文西如何成為一位偉大的人
3. 下列關於文藝復興時期的敘述，何者不正確？
　(A) 該時期意指「誕生」。

(B) 該時期從十四世紀延續到十七世紀。
(C) 那是個科學和藝術領域充滿創意的時期。
(D) 當時的博學之士渴望認識世界。
4. 第二段中的「inspire」意思近於＿＿＿＿＿。
　(A) 收集　　　　　　(B) 改善
　(C) 激勵　　　　　(D) 使感興趣
5. 根據本文，下列何者正確？
　(A) 達文西是飛行機器的發明者。
　(B) 達文西大部分的計畫都成為了真實的機器。
　(C) 達文西用他的天賦顯示了人類能如何有力地思考和行動。
　(D) 伊格・塞考斯基是現代坦克車的發明者。

🍷 Try it!

1. creativity　2. gift　　3. the heavens
4. future　　5. original

---

creativity　n.　創意
gift　n.　天份
the heavens　n.　天空

future　n.　未來
original　adj.　原始的
rebirth　n.　重生

the Renaissance　n.　文藝復興
helicopter　n.　直昇機
humankind　n.　人類

45 減重大作戰！
Keep the Pounds Off!

　　每年大約都有 7,000 萬美國人試圖減重，全國幾乎每三人中就有一人這麼做。有些人會節食，減少餐後甜點或油膩食物的份量，有些人則會慢跑或到健身中心運動，另外還有些人甚至會去動整形手術。顯然地，減重意味著一大堆苦工，同時也會花上許多金錢。現在你可能會想，為什麼會有這麼多美國人要費心減重？

　　這一切都跟「保持完美體態」有關。對許多人而言，「好看」的同義字就是「瘦」。而其他人則是在聽過許多有關肥胖的負面新聞後，想要讓自己更健康。

　　幾乎每個人都想知道又快又簡單的減重方式，曾被寫過的減肥指南可以擺滿好幾個書架，目的就是為了幫助那些渴望擺脫幾磅肉的人。

　　減重的花費可能極高。健身中心如位於加州奧克蘭的「第一俱樂部」提供團體及個人的訓練課程，會員每天付的費用可能就高達數百美元。他們通常大量運動及少量進食。一位名為路意絲的女士就表示，她在加入這類課程的第 5 天就減掉了 5 磅體重，平均每磅花了她大概 300 塊美金，但她說：「很值得。」

1. 本文主要是關於 ＿＿＿＿＿。
　　(A) 節食
　　(B) 運動
　　(C) 保持完美體態
　　(D) 整形手術
　　→ 選項 A、B 太狹隘，選項 D 較無關。
2. 下列何者有助於減重？
　　(A) 少量進食。
　　(B) 規律運動。
　　(C) 減少甜點或油膩食物的份量。
　　(D) 以上皆是。
3. 人們為何想要減重？
　　(A) 因為很多人都這麼做。
　　(B) 因為他們想要變得好看。
　　(C) 因為那會花掉他們許多錢。
　　(D) 因為他們不想接受整形手術。
4. 第二段中「obesity」意思是非常 ＿＿＿＿＿，而且是一種不健康的方式。
　　(A) 肥胖　　　　　(B) 瘦
　　(C) 瘦到皮包骨　　(D) 苗條
　　→ obesity 表示「過胖」。
5. 以下敘述何者正確？
　　(A) 健身中心只提供團體訓練課程。
　　(B) 減重需要許多的努力與大量的金錢。
　　(C) 幾乎沒什麼書能告訴人們如何減重。
　　(D) 名叫路意絲的女士認為減重花了她太多錢。

🎆 Try it!
1. bother　　2. obviously　3. up to
4. surgery　　5. greasy

---

bother　v.　費心	greasy　adj.　油膩的	cut back　縮減
obviously　adv.　明顯地	surgery　n.　手術	dessert　n.　點心
up to　(數量) 可達到…	go on a diet　節食	costly　adj.　昂貴的

壓垮駱駝的一根稻草
The Straw That Breaks the Camel's Back

曾經有一名阿拉伯人騎著駱駝橫越沙漠。日落之後，他停下來搭起帳棚，生火準備睡覺。

在半睡半醒之間，他感覺帳棚被踢了一下。他轉頭看見駱駝正把頭探進帳棚裡。「拜託您，我的頭必須待在帳棚裡才能保暖，外面太冷了。」駱駝哀求道。「請便。」這名好心的阿拉伯人說，然後他就躺回去繼續睡覺。

沒多久，他感覺到帳棚被推了一下。又是駱駝在踢。「主人，」駱駝說，「現在我的頭暖了，但我的脖子仍然很冷。你介意我把脖子也伸進來嗎？」「沒問題。」阿拉伯人回答道。但這次他感覺帳棚裡變得有點擠。

就在他正要睡著的時候，駱駝又踢了帳棚一下。這回，駱駝要求把前腿放進帳棚裡。這名阿拉伯人移動位置挪出空間給駱駝，但帳棚裡已不再舒適了。

此時，駱駝一腳用力踢在阿拉伯人臉上，大叫著，「這帳棚太小，擠不下我們兩個。你給我滾出帳棚！」說完，駱駝就重重地一腳把那名可憐的阿拉伯人踢飛了。

1. 下列何諺語可作為故事總結？
 (A) 眼見為憑。　　(B) 欲速則不達。
 (C) 惡有惡報。　　**(D) 得寸進尺。**

2. 從故事上下文我們可以推斷，日落後天氣是 _____ 的。
 (A) 炎熱　(B) 多風　(C) 多雨　**(D) 寒冷**
 → 答題關鍵 freezing 表示「極冷的」，相當於 chilly。

3. 為什麼駱駝一再踢帳棚？
 (A) 因為牠怕黑。
 (B) 因為那名阿拉伯人對牠很壞。
 (C) 因為牠想叫醒那名阿拉伯人。
 (D) 因為牠想把帳棚據為己有。

4. 第二段出現的片語「be my guest」意指 _____。
 (A) 感到舒適和放鬆
 (B) 不願意和某人分享某物
 (C) 被邀請參加活動最重要的人物
 (D) 許可某人做他或她所要求的事
 → be my guest 表示「請便；別客氣」。

5. 這篇文章很可能出自於 _____。
 (A) 一本科學期刊　　**(B) 一本故事書**
 (C) 一本電腦雜誌　　(D) 一份學術報告
 → 從駱駝被擬人化，可推知此文章是則故事。

Try it!
1. freezing　　2. get lost　　3. make room
4. put up　　5. is about to

---

freezing　adj.　極冷的
get lost　滾開
make room　挪出空間
put up　安置

be about to　即將…
camel　n.　駱駝
desert　n.　沙漠
kick　n.　踢

beg　v.　乞求
master　n.　主人
crowded　adj.　擁擠的
no longer　不再

47 群眾募資的挑戰
The Challenges of Crowdfunding

準備好要將你的偉大想法轉變為真正的業務了嗎？找到合適的資金對於成功至關重要。群眾募資是企業家為他們的新創公司募集資金的一種方式。但這並不總是那麼容易。讓我們來探討會遇到的挑戰以及克服的方法吧。

其中一項挑戰是讓人們對你的公司感興趣，並滿足他們的期待。有些投資人可能只看到未來，而不關心你的新創公司至今表現如何，所以他們可能對你期待過高。要解決這個問題，請清楚說明你公司的情況以及你的產品如何運作。

另一個挑戰是並非所有投資人都知道群眾募資如何運作。他們一開始可能不信任你。你可以深入了解你的業務，並解釋他們為什麼應該投資你的新創公司，藉此來解決這個問題。

此外，決定募集多少資金也可能很棘手。這不僅關係到你的需求，也關係到公司的價值。與先前有此經驗的其他人聊聊，以獲取想法。注意不要要求太多。

再者，群眾募資的平臺很多，但並非全都一樣。有些較適合新興的新創公司，而有些則適合擁有穩定產品的公司。多方嘗試不同的平臺，提出問題，但也不要使用太多。

最後，確保你的想法安全很重要。投資者需要足夠資訊來了解你的新創公司，但不要提供他們超出他們所需的量。運用著作權法保護你的部分想法，並讓人們簽署不洩露重要資訊的協議。

如果你了解這些挑戰並做好充分的準備，你為新創公司募集資金時，就能有更好的表現。祝你好運！

1. 這篇文章的主旨為何？
   (A) 找到合適資金的重要性。
   (B) 新創公司進行群眾募資的挑戰與解決之道。
   (C) 探索不同的商業模式。
   (D) 著作權法如何保障新創公司的想法。

2. 根據本文，當你讓人們對你的公司感興趣時，可能會面臨什麼挑戰？
   (A) 投資人期待太高。
   (B) 缺乏優良的商業模式。
   (C) 不了解人們要什麼。
   (D) 選擇適合的平臺。

3. 從關於該為新創公司募集多少資金的建議，可以推論出下列何者？
   (A) 永遠要要求比實際需要的更多。
   (B) 公司的價值與此無關。
   (C) 你的需求決定了一切。
   (D) 向有經驗的人尋求忠告。

4. 作者如何開始這篇文章？
   (A) 給予定義。　　　　**(B) 提出問題。**
   (C) 提供統計數據。　　(D) 比較人們的反應。

5. 下列何者最能描述作者對群眾募資未來的態度？
   (A) 感到驚豔。　　　　(B) 懷抱疑慮。
   (C) 抱持希望。　　　(D) 保守以對。

> **Try it!**
> 1. challenge　2. expectation　3. invest
> 4. platforms　5. reveal

challenge n. 挑戰	platform n. 平臺	startup n. 新創公司
expectation n. 期待	reveal v. 洩露；顯露	copyright n. 著作權
invest v. 投資	crucial adj. 重要的	tricky adj. 棘手的

48 等一下，我需要買這樣東西嗎？
Wait a Minute. Do I Need to Buy This?

當你在超市排隊結帳時，注意到結帳櫃臺附近有些巧克力棒，一個牌子上寫著這些是新產品，所以你拿了幾條。接著，你也買了一些口香糖，它們正在打折，此外還為孩子買了幾樣玩具。當你回到家時，發現自己買下原本不在購物清單上的東西，而且由於衝動購物，你花了超出預算的錢。

當人們基於衝動而購買，就叫做衝動購物。這些物品往往被放在店內前方展示台上，更常見於消費者排隊等待結帳的櫃臺附近。一些常見的衝動購物包括糖果、巧克力、口香糖、玩具等。

衝動購物通常是極短時間內做下的決定。店家利用特別的展示方式，再加上如「低價促銷」、「免費」以及「打折」等字眼，吸引想要撿便宜的消費者。寫著「限時促銷」或「只有一天」等字樣的牌子，亦會促使消費者作出快速決定。

令人驚訝的是，一份報告顯示，人們在店裡買的東西有高達百分之四十根本不在原本的購物清單上。因此，似乎很清楚的是，只要人們持續衝動購物，店家就會大開方便之門，讓人更容易買下手。

1. 下列何者並非常見的衝動購買之物品？
  (A) 麵包。　　　　　　(B) 糖果。
  (C) 巧克力。　　　　　(D) 口香糖。
2. 根據本篇文章，何謂「衝動購物」？
  (A) 人們買下如巧克力、糖果或玩具等物品。
  (B) 人們看到某物品時就買下來，但原先並未計畫要購買該物品。

(C) 人們逼自己去買一些不喜歡的東西。
(D) 人們以非常低的價格購買物品。
3. 消費者常常在哪裡發現衝動購物？
  (A) 雜誌區。　　　　　(B) 麵包區。
  (C) 結帳櫃臺附近。　　(D) 大型牌子旁邊。
4. 下列關於衝動購物的敘述何者不正確？
  (A) 衝動購買品往往不在消費者的購物清單上。
  (B) 店家會促發衝動購買行為。
  (C) 衝動購物的決定往往在短時間內作出。
  (D) 寫著「只有一天」的牌子並不會促發衝動購物。
5. 在衝動購物前一刻，你心裡的念頭可能會是什麼？
  (A) 「我不能再買東西了，我必須省錢。」
  (B) 「我必須買下這個，它是特價品。」
  (C) 「下次我必須寫個購物清單。」
  (D) 「買下這個之前，我會再次考慮。」

Try it!
1. offer　　2. decision　　3. limited
4. notice　　5. customer

offer v. 提供	customer n. 顧客	display n. 陳列
decision n. 決定	stand in line 排隊	include v. 包含
limited adj. 受限制的	impulse buying 衝動購物	phrase n. 詞組
notice v. 注意	item n. 物品	product n. 產品

49 人生戲法
Juggling Life's Glass and Rubber Balls

　　高德溫教授站在桌子前，桌上擺了幾樣物品：一個玻璃罐、幾顆高爾夫球、一些石頭、沙子和一個馬克杯。首先他將高爾夫球放進罐子裡，並問道：「同學們，這個罐子滿了嗎？」「滿了。」我們都這麼回答。接著他把幾顆小石頭放進罐子裡，填滿了高爾夫球間的間隙。「現在，這個罐子滿了嗎？」高德溫老師又朝我們問了同一個問題。「當然。」我們答道。接著他把沙子倒進罐子裡，又再問一次，而我們說：「它已經滿了。」

　　最後，他將馬克杯斜斜一倒，一種棕色液體立刻流入罐子裡。我們都很好奇那是什麼意思。「現在，」高德溫老師說，「我要你們把這個罐子比做自己的生命。高爾夫球代表最重要的東西：家人、朋友、健康和你的熱情。有了這些，就算其他東西都不見了，你的生命仍是完滿的。這些小石頭就像你的工作、房子和車子，是生命中較不重要的東西，而沙子是瑣碎的小事，一些不重要的東西。」

　　「如果你先把沙子倒進去，」他繼續說，「就沒有空間可放進球或石頭了，這個道理在生命中也一樣。若你陷在一些不重要的事物裡停滯不前，就沒有空間容納重要的東西了。」

　　我舉手問他那種棕色液體是什麼，而且代表什麼。教授笑了，他說，「那是咖啡。意思是，無論日常生活有多忙碌，都總有時間讓你和朋友們喝杯咖啡的。」

1.這篇文章主要是關於如何 _____ 。
　(A) 製作咖啡
　(B) 做一項實驗
　(C) 使一個人的生命完滿
　(D) 處理生命中的瑣碎事物

2.小石頭代表 _____ 。
　(A) 工作　　　　　(B) 家庭
　(C) 朋友　　　　　(D) 以上皆是。

3.在高德溫教授看來，生命中最重要的東西是什麼？
　(A) 健康。　　　　　(B) 熱情。
　(C) 友誼。　　　　　**(D) 以上皆是。**

4.第三段的片語「get stuck on」意指 _____ 。
　(A) 無法從某處脫身
　(B) 無法脫離一個很壞的狀況
　(C) 因為無法擺脫某物而只能保有之
　(D) 陷入停滯狀態難以前進

5.下列敘述何者正確？
　(A) 罐子代表一個人的生命。
　(B) 沙子代表生命中極重要的東西。
　(C) 高爾夫球代表生命中很不重要的東西。
　(D) 一個人的工作、房子和車子是生命中最重要的東西。

Try it!

1. curious　　2. passion　　3. liquid
4. stands for　　5. poured

curious　adj.　好奇的	stand for　代表	mug　n.　馬克杯
passion　n.　熱情	pour　v.　倒出	tilt　v.　傾斜
liquid　n.　液體	jar　n.　玻璃罐	flow　v.　流出

美式英文與英式英文
American vs. British English

美國人和英國人的確都說英文，但在美式英文和英式英文之間也確實有些不同。

首先，它們聽起來就相當不一樣。美國人在說話的時候，喜歡將字連在一起。例如，你可能會聽到美國人說「I gotta go」(我得走了。) 而非「I got to go」，以及「Gotcha!」(瞭解了！) 而不是「Got you!」。相反地，英國人發音就比較清楚明確。

在美式及英式英文裡，同樣的字可能會有不同的意思。而從另一方面來說，不同的字也可能會有相同的意思。在和美國朋友吃完飯後，你會說：「請給我帳單 (check)，好嗎？」但叫來英國服務生時，你會說：「可以請你把帳單 (bill) 給我嗎？」或者，美國人可能會告訴你：「我想去渡假 (vacation)。」而英國人則會用「假日 (holiday)」來代替。

這些所有的差異都可能會令學英文的學生感到不知所措，但並非只有英文如此。說同樣語言的人們，彼此間若不是相鄰而居，就會逐漸養成各自使用語言的習慣。此外，語言就像生物，它們會成長、改變。在不同的土地上，相同的語言就可能以不同的方式產生變化，而英文正是一個完美的例證。

1. 本文主要是關於＿＿＿＿＿。
   (A) 英文在美國的發展
   (B) 英美兩國文化之差異
   (C) 美國人和英國人都說英文的原因
   (D) 美式英文和英式英文的不同
   → 此文章採用破題法，第一段便點出本文主題。

2. 下列何者為美式英文用法？
   (A) 「I gotta go.」　　(B) 「Gotcha!」
   (C) 「Check.」　　**(D) 以上皆是。**

3. 以下敘述何者正確？
   (A) 英國人說話時，會在字與字之間停頓。
   (B) 在美式英文及英式英文中，不同的字可能會有相同的意思。
   (C) 「take a holiday」這個片語經常為美國人所使用。
   (D) 美式英文和英式英文並沒有文法上的差異。

4. 英國人使用以下何者說法？
   (A) 「Stand in line.」
   (B) 「I gotta go.」
   (C) 「Can I have the bill, please?」
   (D) 「I just had a vacation.」

5. 以下敘述何者不正確？
   (A) 在不同的地方，相同的語言可能會有不同的變化。
   (B) 語言絕不會成長或改變。
   (C) 美國人和英國人有時會用不同的用語來指涉相同的事物。
   (D) 在美式英文及英式英文中，相同的字可能會有不同的意思。

Try it!
1. for sure　　2. quite　　3. on the contrary
4. besides　　5. differences

---

for sure	確定	besides	adv.	此外	
quite	adv. 非常地	difference	n.	差異	
on the country	正好相反	link	v.	連接	

distinctly　adv.　清楚地
waiter　n.　服務生
overwhelming　adj.　壓倒性的

核心英文字彙力
2001~4500 隨身讀（三版）

一本在手，核心字彙帶著走！

◆ **符合學測範圍**

依據「高中英文參考詞彙表 (111 學年度起適用)」編寫，收錄 Level 3~5 學測必背單字，共 100 回。掌握核心字彙，備戰學測這本就夠！

◆ **素養例句**

精心編寫多元情境例句，擴大字彙應用，強化學用合一的素養精神。

◆ **補充詳盡**

補充常用搭配詞、同反義字及片語，有利舉一反三、輕鬆延伸學習範圍。

◆ **配套豐富**

(1) 電子朗讀音檔：專業外籍錄音員錄製，音檔採「拼讀」模式 (core，c-o-r-e，core，核心)，用聽覺輔助記憶。

(2) 英文三民誌 2.0 APP：免費下載使用，隨時隨地培養核心英文字彙力。

Intermediate Reading:
英文閱讀 High Five

掌握大考新趨勢，搶先練習新題型！

王隆興 編著

★全書分為5大主題：生態物種、人文歷史、科學科技、環境保育、醫學保健，共50篇由外籍作者精心編寫之文章。

★題目仿111學年度學測參考試卷命題方向設計，為未來大考提前作準備，搶先練習第二部分新題型──混合題。

★隨書附贈解析夾冊，方便練習後閱讀文章中譯及試題解析，並於解析補充每回文章精選的15個字彙。

輕鬆掌握閱讀關鍵　養成優質閱讀能力

★ 精選50篇貼近生活經驗、題材活潑多元的文章，培養閱讀能力。

★ 以初級字彙、句型為主架構文章，奠定基礎閱讀實力。

★ 閱測題目掌握五大閱讀技巧，涵蓋各類考試出題關鍵，訓練綜合運用詞彙、
　 語意、語法知識之能力。

★ Try it! 單元每回精選5組單字或片語，累積讀者字彙實力。

★ 附文章及閱測翻譯、重點試題說明、難字提示，自我評量輕鬆上手。

三民網路書店
www.sanmin.com.tw

「悅讀養成」與
「解析夾冊」不分售
80822G